MY
BIG BOOK
of
STORIES
and
RHYMES

MY
BIG BOOK
of
STORIES
and
RHYMES

Ladybird

Stories and rhymes in this book were previously published by Ladybird Books Ltd in *Animal Stories, Teddy Bear Tales, Nursery Rhymes* and *Stories for Bedtime*.

All Ladybird books are available at most bookshops, supermarkets and newsagents, or can be ordered direct from:
Ladybird Postal Sales PO Box 133 Paignton TQ3 2YP England
Telephone: (+44) 01803 554761 *Fax:* (+44) 01803 663394

A catalogue record for this book is available from the British Library

Published by Ladybird Books Ltd
A subsidiary of the Penguin Group
A Pearson Company
© LADYBIRD BOOKS LTD MCMXCVIII
Birthday Bear © Georgina Russell

LADYBIRD and the device of a Ladybird are trademarks of Ladybird Books Ltd Loughborough Leicestershire UK

Contents

Credits

Teddy Bear Tales
Chosen by Ronne Randall

Animal Stories
Chosen by Ronne Randall

Nursery Rhymes
Chosen by Ronne Randall

Nursery Tales
Chosen by Tony Bradman
Retold by Brian Morse

Illustrated by Peter Stevenson

TEDDY BEAR
TALES

About the stories...

Teddy bears are special friends for children
everywhere. They are held close at bedtime, taken
on holidays and journeys, and share children's secrets,
worries and dreams. And as all children know, teddy
bears have lots of adventures. The fourteen stories and
five rhymes that follow feature all sorts of teddy bears—
mischievous bears, sporty bears, hungry bears, bears who
smile (and some who don't!)—and one extra special
Christmas bear.

Contents

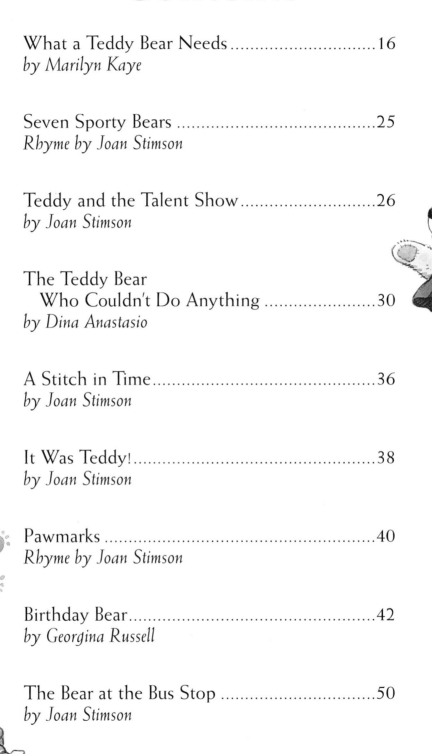

What a Teddy Bear Needs

In a toy shop, on a shelf, sat a row of brand-new teddy bears. They all had fluffy brown fur. They all had big button noses. They all had bright red ribbons round their necks. And they were all smiling.

Except for Eddy Teddy. Eddy Teddy never smiled.

"You need to smile," the other bears told him. "If you don't smile, no one will ever want to take you home."

"I don't need to smile," Eddy said proudly. "I have the fluffiest fur and the biggest nose and the brightest ribbon. I'm the finest teddy bear in this shop."

Just then, a little boy and his mother came into the shop. All the teddy bears sat up straight and smiled their biggest smiles. All except Eddy Teddy. He just sat there.

"I want that one," the little boy told his mother. He pointed to the bear just to the left of Eddy.

What a silly boy, thought Eddy. *I've got fluffier fur than that bear!*

Then a little girl and her father came into the shop. "Please, may I have that bear?" she asked her father. She pointed to the bear just to the right of Eddy.

What a foolish girl, thought Eddy. *That bear's nose is much smaller than mine!*

More and more boys and girls came into the shop. One by one, they each picked a teddy bear. But no one picked Eddy Teddy. Soon he was all alone on the shelf.

I'm not going to sit here and wait any longer, Eddy decided. *I'll go out and find someone to take me home!*

He hopped down from the shelf and left the shop.

Across the road, there was a big park where boys and girls were playing. Eddy saw one little boy playing with a very old teddy bear.

"Hello," said Eddy, walking right up to the boy. "My name is Eddy Teddy, and I will be your new bear."

"No, thank you," said the little boy. "I already have a teddy bear."

"But I'm a much better teddy bear!" Eddy said. "I have the fluffiest fur and the biggest nose and the brightest ribbon. I'm the finest teddy bear in the world!"

"But my teddy bear has something you don't have," said the boy. And he walked away, hugging his old teddy bear.

Then Eddy saw another little boy playing with a tatty old teddy bear.

"Hello," said Eddy. "Wouldn't you like a nice new teddy bear?"

"No, thank you," the boy said. "I'm happy with my own teddy bear."

"But your teddy bear doesn't have fluffy fur, or a big button nose, or a red ribbon," Eddy told him.

"I don't care," the boy said. "He's got something better."

Then Eddy saw a little girl playing all alone. She was the prettiest girl Eddy had ever seen. She had yellow hair and big blue eyes. He hurried over to her.

"Hello," said Eddy. "Do you want a teddy bear?"

"Yes, I do," said the little girl.

"Well, here I am!" said Eddy.

"No, thank you," the little girl said. "You're not the right teddy bear for me."

"Why not?" asked Eddy. "I have the fluffiest fur and the biggest nose and the brightest ribbon!"

"But you don't have what a teddy bear really needs," the little girl said sadly.

Eddy was puzzled. He was sure he had everything a teddy bear needed.

Then Eddy saw a rose bush. *That must be what I need,* he thought. *A big red rose for my bright red ribbon.* So he jumped into the rose bush to get the biggest rose.

"Ouch! Ouch! Help!" The thorns pricked Eddy all over. He was stuck inside the bush and he couldn't get out.

The little girl with the yellow hair grabbed Eddy's ears and pulled him free.

"Oh, dear," she said. "You've lost your button nose."

That wasn't all. Stuck to the thorns were bits and pieces of Eddy's fur. And waving from a branch was his bright red ribbon.

"Oh, no!" Eddy cried. He turned away from the little girl and ran all the way back to the toy shop.

On the shelf sat a row of brand-new teddy bears. When they saw Eddy, they shook their heads. "You look terrible!" they said.

Eddy wanted to cry. Now no one would ever want to take him home.

Just then the shop door opened. In walked the yellow-haired little girl with her mother.

All the teddy bears sat up straight and smiled. Except for Eddy Teddy. He hung his head in shame.

22

"Hello," said the little girl.

Eddy looked up. The little girl was standing right in front of him. She smiled.

And Eddy couldn't help himself. He smiled right back.

"That's the teddy bear I want," the little girl said.

Her mother was surprised. "But he doesn't have fluffy fur or a red ribbon or a button nose," she said. "Why do you want him?"

"Because he has the nicest smile," the little girl said, taking Eddy down from the shelf.

Then Eddy knew what a teddy bear really needs. A teddy bear doesn't need the fluffiest fur or the biggest nose or the brightest ribbon. All a teddy bear needs is a great big smile.

And as the little girl hugged him tightly, Eddy Teddy knew that he would go on smiling for ever.

Seven Sporty Bears

Monday's bear runs far and wide,
Tuesday's bear can bike and ride.

Wednesday's bear plays ball with me,
Thursday's bear can climb a tree.

Friday's bear *will* jump in puddles,
Saturday's bear is best at cuddles.

But Sunday's bear, I'm proud to say,
Has just scored a goal…
Hip, hip, HOORAY!

Teddy and the Talent Show

Teddy and Tom were excited. They were about to watch a talent show.

"I do hope there'll be a trick cyclist," said Tom.

Well, I want to see some real magic, thought Teddy. And he peered out from his tip-up seat.

The first act was a group of singers. They were very good, and Teddy tapped his paw while Tom hummed to the music.

Next came a comedian. Tom couldn't stop laughing at the jokes. And Teddy nearly fell off his seat.

Then Tom got his wish, and a trick cyclist sped onto the stage.

"Wow!" whispered Tom. "I can barely balance on two wheels, let alone one."

And I still need three and a knee, thought Teddy.

The next act was a troupe of dancers. Teddy and Tom looked at each other and yawned. But there was still one act to follow.

"Now, last," boomed the voice of the presenter, "but by no means least," he added cheerfully, "I give you… *Malcolm the Magician!*"

Teddy sat bolt upright. And when Malcolm asked for a volunteer from the audience, somehow Teddy's arm shot up with all the rest.

Malcolm pretended to take a long time choosing. "The young man in the striped dungarees," he announced at last.

First Teddy was put in a special box.

"Ooooooh," went the audience. It looked just as if Malcolm was sawing Teddy in two!

Then he made him disappear...

and reappear with a rabbit.

In fact, Teddy helped Malcolm with all his tricks. At the end of the act the applause was deafening.

That night Mum asked Tom if he had enjoyed the show.

"Oh, Mum," cried Tom, "it was... *magic!*"

And Teddy couldn't help but agree.

The Teddy Bear
Who Couldn't Do Anything

The teddy bear rested his head on the pillow and looked at the toy shelf. The other toys didn't say hello, or smile, or even nod. They never paid any attention to him. They thought he was just a silly old bear who didn't know how to do anything.

Perhaps they're right, thought the teddy bear, looking at the other toys. *The soldier knows how to march. The ballerina knows how to dance. The monkey can play the drum. But all I can do is lie here.*

Up on the shelf, the soldier was getting ready to march. He straightened his shoulders and stood tall as he stepped forward.

The teddy bear watched the shiny soldier march proudly across the shelf. He swung his arms and tapped his heels and turned smartly each time he came to the edge.

"Perhaps I can stand straight and tall and march like the soldier," said the teddy bear, sitting up. "In fact, I'm *sure* I can."

The toy soldier stopped marching and stared at the bear. "What did you say?" he asked.

"Well," said the teddy bear quietly, because suddenly he wasn't so sure of himself, "I could try."

The teddy bear rolled off the bed and tried to march. But his legs were too fat and his tummy was too big. He took three small steps and fell down.

The other toys laughed as the bear climbed back onto the bed.

Then the ballerina began to dance. Round and round she twirled.

The teddy bear tried to dance like the ballerina, but he was much too clumsy. He fell down with a thud, and felt very foolish indeed.

There must be something I can do, the teddy bear thought as he pulled himself back onto the bed. But as hard as he tried, he couldn't think of a single thing.

Just then the monkey stepped forward and started to play his drum. *Tap, tap,* went the drum. *Tap, tap, tap, tap, tap, tap.*

The teddy bear sat up and listened. "I can do that," he said. "I can make a drumming sound like that."

He went to the toybox and pulled out two drumsticks. Then he closed the lid and wrapped his paws round the sticks.

Tap, tap, went the drumsticks on the toybox lid. The teddy bear smiled. At last he had found something he could do.

But then the sticks slid out of his fat little paws and fell to the floor.

The teddy bear shook his head and sat down in the corner.
"It's no use," he sighed. "I really can't do anything special."

He sat in the corner for a long time, while the other toys marched
and played and danced. Then he climbed back into bed and slid
down under the covers.

When the sun set and the room grew dark, the little soldier led
the ballerina and the monkey back to their places on the shelf.
Soon it would be time for the boy to come into the room.

At last the boy turned on the light.
He walked over to the toy shelf.

The soldier stood tall and proud.

The monkey held his drumsticks tightly.

The ballerina was on her toes, ready to dance.

But the boy shook his head. He walked over to the bed and looked on his pillow. Then he looked under the bed. The boy's face grew worried and sad.

Finally the boy got into bed. But he couldn't sleep. Something was wrong.

And then the boy's toe felt something – something soft and round and fat and nice. He reached down, deep under the covers, and found… his teddy bear.

The boy hugged the bear and was happy.

And the bear who couldn't do anything but hug was happy, too.

A Stitch in Time

"Cheer up, Teddy!" began Rabbit.

"It's a lovely, sunny day," went on Dog.

"And you should be happy!" finished Cat.

"But I *am* happy," Teddy told them. "It's just that my mouth turns down at the corners. And I can't do anything about it."

"Good heavens!" cried Cat. *She* had a smile as wide as her face.

"Do you mean you were *made* that way?" grinned Dog and Rabbit together.

Teddy nodded sadly. "However happy I feel inside," he explained, "I always *look* miserable. If only I had just a small smile, then I'm sure Boy would spend more time with me."

That night, when Teddy was asleep, Rabbit, Dog and Cat lay awake. At last they came up with a plan.

Next day they told Teddy what he must do.

"Will it hurt?" he asked.

Rabbit, Dog and Cat shook their heads. "Not much," they said.

After supper Boy had his bath.

"Just look at this T-shirt!" cried his mum. "It's almost torn in half."

And with that, she opened the bathroom door and threw the T-shirt across the hallway. It landed in the mending pile.

"*Now!*" cried Rabbit, Dog and Cat.

Teddy leaned over the edge of the bed. "*Ouch!*" He bounced onto the floor, across the hallway and straight on top of the mending pile.

When Boy woke up next morning, Teddy was propped up at the end of his bed. Rabbit, Dog and Cat grinned and waited.

"And what are *you* smiling about?" Boy asked Teddy.

Teddy didn't say a word. He just smiled back.

"Come on," cried Boy suddenly. He grabbed Teddy and leapt out of bed.

"It's a lovely, sunny day. And we're going to play outside together… *all morning!*"

It Was Teddy!

Carl was a careless little boy. But he didn't like to admit it.

So, when he turned on the taps and flooded the bathroom, he wouldn't own up. "It was Teddy!" he told his parents.

The same thing happened when Carl took an ice cream out of the freezer, and then left it to melt.

"What a waste!" said Mum.

"What a *careless* Teddy!" sighed Carl.

Then one day Carl accidentally hurled a ball through Mrs Weaver's window.

"*Naughty* Teddy!" announced naughty Carl.

"Teddy has been causing a *lot* of trouble," said Dad. So he decided to have a talk with Carl's teacher.

Now, Carl and Teddy were still new boys at school. But Carl enjoyed school, and he worked hard.

"Next week," Miss Mulberry told the children, "we are having an important visitor. I want you all to make her a nice picture."

Carl painted his best picture ever. Miss Mulberry put it up on the wall along with the others.

When the important visitor arrived, she was impressed. "What wonderful paintings!" she exclaimed. Then she took a closer look and pointed to Carl's. "Who painted *this* one?" she asked. "It's outstanding!"

Carl squirmed with pride, and Miss Mulberry smiled across the room. "It was Teddy!" she told the visitor.

That evening Carl took a glass of milk up to his bedroom. But he soon came down again.

"Sorry, " said Carl. "I've spilt my milk and made a mess."

Mum and Dad looked amazed. "Who taught you to own up?" they asked.

Carl beamed at his parents. Then he told them, "It was Teddy!"

Pawmarks

There are pawmarks on the table,
There are pawmarks on the chairs.
There are pawmarks in the hallway,
As well as up the stairs!

There are pawmarks in the bathroom,
There are pawmarks on the mat.
There are pawmarks on the aftershave –
Dad won't think much of *that*!

There are pawmarks in the bedroom,
There are pawmarks in the bed.
There are pawmarks on my nightie
In several shades of red.

Now, each and every pawmark
Came from a bear called Sid –
And all because the finger paints
Were left without a lid!

Birthday Bear

"That's the end of your story, Sally," said Mum. "Now snuggle down with Bear and go to sleep."

"I'm too excited to sleep," said Sally. "I can't wait until tomorrow."

"I know," said Mum. "There are going to be lots of surprises."

Bear listened with sudden interest. Surprises! He liked surprises, too.

Sally lay awake for a long time, tossing and turning and thinking and wondering. But at last she drifted off to sleep.

Bear, however, was still doing a lot of thinking and wondering of his own.

As soon as everyone was asleep, Bear slipped out of Sally's arms and slid down onto the floor.

"I'll start with the cupboard under the stairs," he said to himself. "That's a good hiding place for surprises."

It was dark and crowded in the cupboard, so Bear had to rummage around with his paws.

"Coats and scarves, boots and shoes, cans of old paint, umbrellas…" he muttered. "But no sign of any surprises."

He rummaged some more.

"Brushes and brooms, a teapot, a beach ball, an old hat… Oh! And a big parcel wrapped in pretty paper and tied with a ribbon!"

Bear paused…

"A parcel… Parcels mean presents, and presents mean surprises. So this must be a surprise," he decided.

He looked longingly at the parcel, wondering what was inside. But he didn't open it. "If I open it, it won't be a surprise any longer," he said to himself. So, reluctantly, he turned away from the cupboard.

"Perhaps I'll look in the kitchen next," he decided. "There may be an eating sort of surprise in there."

In the kitchen, Bear tried the cupboards first.

"Pots and pans, bowls and plates, cups and saucers, but no surprises," he said sadly to himself.

He tried the fridge next.

"Butter and milk, yogurt and eggs, tomatoes and lettuce… Oh! And a huge cake covered in pink icing, with sugar teddies dancing round the side!"

44

Bear thought for a moment. "A special cake… Special cakes with pink icing mean special occasions, and special occasions mean surprises. So this *must* be a surprise!" he decided.

But Bear was puzzled. *What is the special occasion?* he wondered.

Bear thought and thought. "I give up," he said to himself at last. "I'd better look in the dining room next. There may be a clue in there."

Bear pushed open the door and looked around.

"Table and chairs, knives and forks, plates and glasses. No surprises here."

He looked again.

"Oh! And balloons and funny hats!"

Bear thought for a moment. "Balloons and funny hats mean parties," he told himself, "and parties mean special occasions, and special occasions mean surprises. But *what* is the special occasion?"

Bear sat down and thought even harder. *It can't be Christmas – I haven't seen a Christmas tree...*

He thought some more. *I wonder if it's... could it be...?* Suddenly Bear tingled with excitement.

"Yes! That's it!" he said, jumping up. "It must be... it's got to be... my birthday! And Sally and her mum want it to be a surprise for me!"

Bear smiled a big smile as he climbed the stairs. *I'd better go to bed now*, he thought. *Tomorrow is going to be a big day for me.*

Next afternoon, Bear watched as Sally put on her party dress and party shoes. He was bursting with anticipation.

My big moment, thought Bear as Sally carried him downstairs.

The dining room was full of children wearing the funny hats and playing with the balloons. Oh! And there on the table Bear could see the wrapped-up present. Next to it was the cake with the pink icing and the sugar teddies dancing round the side.

That's funny! thought Bear, as he counted the candles on the cake. *I didn't know I was five.*

At that moment, all the children started singing:

> *"Happy birthday to you,*
> *Happy birthday to you."*

Bear listened happily.

> *"Happy birthday, dear Sally,*
> *Happy birthday to you!"*

Bear couldn't believe his ears. It was *Sally's* birthday, not his. This was the wrong sort of surprise! It was awful.

All the children were laughing and shouting. Sally was smiling. Bear felt disappointed, sad and forgotten.

Then all at once Sally announced, "I'm going to blow out the candles. And my special friend Bear is going to help me." She tied the pink ribbon from the parcel in a big bow round his neck, and gave him a pink party hat.

Bear brightened up. He hadn't been forgotten after all!

Sally took a big breath. So did Bear. All five candles went out with one puff.

Or was it two?

"Happy birthday, Sally!" cried the children. "Well done, Bear!"

Bear grinned to himself. He felt very smart in his party hat and bow. And he felt proud to be Sally's special friend. It was a happy surprise after all.

The Bear at the Bus Stop

"Look, Dad," cried the girl. "Someone's left their teddy at the bus stop."

"So they have," said Dad. "Do you think we should take him home with us?"

"Oh no!" cried the girl. "What if his owner comes back and Teddy isn't here?"

Just then the bus came. And the girl and her dad disappeared.

Before the next bus came, a lady came along. She was on her way to a jumble sale.

"Wouldn't you look nice on my Book and Toy Stall!" she told Teddy. But then she thought again.

"I'm sure your owner will be here very soon," she said. "So here's one of my books to sit on, to make you more comfortable while you wait."

50

51

Before the next bus, a childminder arrived. The children she was looking after squealed and pointed. "I want that bear!" they cried together.

But the childminder was firm. "That bear belongs to someone else," she said. "But I'm sure he won't mind if we read his book while we wait."

The children enjoyed Teddy's book so much that they left him one of their chewy chocolate bars.

Before the next bus, three big boys came along.

"Hey," one of them cried. "Here's a bear we can chuck around on the bus!"

The biggest boy made a grab for Teddy.
Whoops! Off came Teddy's arm.

"How was I supposed to know his arm was loose?" complained the biggest boy. And he delved into his pocket for his Wonder Knife.

Carefully and very gently, the biggest boy put Teddy back together. "Better than he was in the first place!" he beamed.

All day long the people who met Teddy wondered if he would be all right. When they got off the bus that evening, they couldn't wait to see if he was still there.

"Oh!" they all said in turn. "He's gone!"

But then they spotted a note:

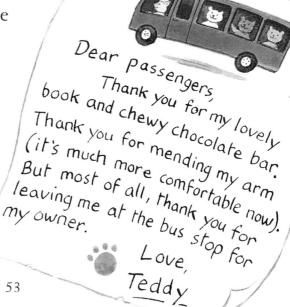

Dear passengers,
Thank you for my lovely book and chewy chocolate bar. Thank you for mending my arm (it's much more comfortable now). But most of all, thank you for leaving me at the bus stop for my owner.
Love,
Teddy

53

No Fun Fair for Freddy

Pippa and Freddy went almost everywhere together.

But Pippa was a girl who easily became excited and... forgetful!

"Where's Freddy?" Mum would say at bedtime. And then there would be a frantic search.

Freddy had been left everywhere, from the library to the swimming pool.

In the end, Mum made him a special badge. On it were his name, address and telephone number. And kind people were always either delivering Freddy to the door or telephoning for him to be collected.

One day, Pippa was particularly excited. A fun fair was coming to town the following week! But, right from the start, Mum was firm.

"No fun fair for Freddy," she announced. "It wouldn't be safe. It wouldn't be sensible. Freddy might get lost or squashed in no time at all."

All week Pippa argued. And the day before the fun fair, she decided to make a *huge* effort.

"If I show Mum that I can be really responsible," Pippa told herself, "then perhaps Freddy can come to the fun fair after all."

That afternoon, Pippa, Freddy and Mum set off for the shops. On the way, they delivered a parcel to Mike's mum.

"Come in," she said. "Mike's building a spaceship."

Pippa clutched Freddy firmly as she raced up the stairs.

"Oooh!" squealed Pippa, when she saw the kit. "Can I help?"

The two friends had a terrific time together. But just as Mum and Pippa were leaving, Mike's mum came running after them.

"Don't forget Freddy," she cried kindly, "or he might fly to the moon without you!"

Pippa blushed. Mum didn't say a word. But Pippa knew exactly what she was thinking: "No fun fair for Freddy!"

When they reached the supermarket, it was even busier than usual. While Mum pushed the trolley, Pippa gave all her attention to Freddy.

But just before the checkout there was a special display.

"Oooh!" squealed Pippa. "It's my favourite snack!" And she rushed forward to load the trolley.

Pippa and Mum chatted happily as they left the store. But suddenly the manager came running after them.

"Don't forget your teddy," he cried kindly, "or he might eat too many Crunchy Crisp-O-s!"

Mum didn't say a word. But Pippa muttered miserably, "No fun fair for Freddy!"

On the way home, Pippa, Freddy and Mum stopped off at the park.

Pippa pushed Freddy carefully on the swings. They whizzed down the slide in a bear hug.

But suddenly Pippa caught sight of Katie.

"Oooh!" squealed Pippa. "Do you want to play hide-and-seek with me?"

At last Mum and Pippa waved goodbye. But then a big boy came running after them.

"Hey!" he called. "Don't forget your bear, or he might get trampled in our game!"

When they got home, Pippa threw herself on her bed. "I don't want to go to the fun fair," she wailed. "Not without Freddy!"

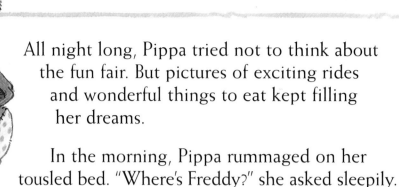

All night long, Pippa tried not to think about the fun fair. But pictures of exciting rides and wonderful things to eat kept filling her dreams.

In the morning, Pippa rummaged on her tousled bed. "Where's Freddy?" she asked sleepily.

And then Pippa saw him.

Freddy was perched on the shelf, looking pleased with himself. He was smartly dressed… in Pippa's old baby sling!

"One of my better brain waves," said Mum, smiling proudly.

And, as soon as she had adjusted the straps to fit Pippa perfectly, Freddy was… all set for the fun fair!

My Bear

I'd like to be a pilot
And hurtle through the air,
But even if I looped the loop,
I still would need my bear.

I'd like to be a jockey
And ride a frisky mare,
But even if I won the race
I still would need my bear.

I'd like to be a gymnast
And dangle for a dare,
But even if I wowed the crowd,
I still would need my bear.

I'd like to be a pop star
With rings and purple hair,
But even if I made you scream,
I still would need my bear.

I'd like to be a teacher–
What lessons I'd prepare!
But even if I knew it all,
I still would need my bear.

It's fun to plan and daydream,
It's better still to share.
So even when he's old and worn,
I still will need my bear.

My Owner

My owner has a rumply bed;
She sometimes doesn't wash!
But even when she snores or squirms,
I never mind a squash.

"Let's play a game," she sometimes cries,
And, "Teddy, you begin."
But sometimes when we play a game,
I *wish* she'd let me win!

My owner sometimes stamps and shouts
(She's not a pretty sight!),
But even when the grown-ups glare,
I'm there to hold her tight.

My owner likes to go on trips
By boat or train or bus.
And if I didn't go as well,
I know there'd be a fuss.

We have our ups and downs of days,
But still we both agree,
I wouldn't change her for the world,
And nor would she change me.

Marcus and Lionel

Marcus and Lionel had been together for as long as they could remember. They lived on the little girl's bed, propped up against her pillow.

Marcus often went places with the little girl. And when he got home, he always told Lionel about his adventures. Lionel was too big to travel, and never got to go anywhere. Sometimes he wished he could have an adventure of his own, but most of the time he was content to sit on the bed and hear about the world outside.

One summer morning, there was lots of bustle and clatter in the house. People had come with boxes for packing things, and there was a van to take everything away. The little girl and her parents were moving to the countryside.

Marcus was going to ride in the car. But Lionel was packed in a box, along with the pillows and some blankets. He just had time to say goodbye to Marcus before the lid was shut.

Marcus had a wonderful journey. There was so much to see! They rode through busy city streets, one after the other.

Then they came to a big bridge. Marcus had never seen a bridge before. *Wait until I tell Lionel about this!* he thought.

As they crossed the bridge, Marcus saw boats in the water. When they got to the other side, he saw hills and a windmill and cows in fields.

I can't wait to tell Lionel! he thought.

At last they arrived at the new house. There were trees at the front, and swings and a slide at the back. The little girl's bedroom looked out over a garden with red roses growing in it.

Lionel and I will be happy here, Marcus thought.

The little girl and her parents started to unpack the boxes. Marcus could hardly wait to see Lionel.

They unpacked the little girl's clothes, and all her books. They unpacked her doll's house and her cowboy hat and boots. There was no sign of Lionel yet.

They unpacked the tea set, the easel and the bedside lamp. There was still no sign of Lionel.

There was only one box left. *Lionel* has *to be in that one,* Marcus thought.

But he wasn't. It was only the little girl's games and jigsaws.

That night, the little girl had to sleep with her mother's pillow—and no Lionel. She hugged Marcus extra tight, and Marcus tried hard to hug her back.

"I'm sure Lionel will turn up," he thought. But Lionel didn't.

Over the next few days, Marcus and the little girl had lots of new things to explore. There were trees to climb, and a little stream with frogs and fish. There was a hidey-hole in one of the big trees, and there were four cats next door who came to visit.

Discovering it all should have been a great adventure for Marcus, but it wasn't much fun. Lionel wasn't there to hear about it when Marcus came home.

The days seemed very long.

One day, the little girl took Marcus out to the car. She and her mum were going to visit someone in the city, and Marcus was going, too.

On the way, Marcus saw lots of things he remembered from the moving day. That made him miss Lionel more than ever.

When they got to the city, the little girl carried Marcus in her usual way—by one arm. This always gave Marcus an interesting view of things.

And that day Marcus got a *very* interesting view of something. Behind an iron gate, on the lawn in front of a big grey building, there were tables with all sorts of things set out on display: chairs and clothes and clocks and books…

And right there, on one of those tables, was… could it be?

Yes! It was… Lionel!

Marcus had to make the little girl stop, so she would see Lionel, too. But how? She and her mum seemed to be in such a hurry!

There was only one way. Gathering all his strength, Marcus stuck out one leg – just far enough to get his foot caught in the gate.

As the little girl walked on, Marcus's foot began to tear. It hurt terribly. But it would be worth it, if only…

"Mum, wait," said the little girl, stopping. "Marcus's foot is stuck."

As the little girl began to free his foot, she suddenly saw what Marcus had seen.

"Mum!" she cried. "Mum, look! It's Lionel! We found him, Mum! We found Lionel!"

Indeed they had. He was a bit dusty, and one of his seams was torn, but otherwise he was fine. They got him from the jumble sale, and that afternoon they took him home to the countryside.

The little girl's mum mended his seam and gave him a bath. She mended Marcus's foot, too, so it didn't hurt any more.

Marcus and Lionel were so happy to be together again. They spent days and days catching up on all that had happened. It was just like old times.

Well, almost: now Lionel had some adventures to tell Marcus about, too!

Edward's First Party

Edward stood on his head. Next he turned a cartwheel. Then he simply sat on his bed and squirmed.

Tomorrow Edward was going to his first Teddy Bear Party.

Fabulous food! Great games! And lots of new bears to meet! he thought to himself.

But then Edward gave a little frown. Because Edward's owner, Tina, had been invited, too. And Tina had *terrible* table manners.

Edward began to fret.

"What if Tina rushes at her food? What if she chatters with her mouth full? And what if... oh no!..." Edward blushed at the thought. *What if Tina gets her horrible hiccups?*

Next morning Edward woke up feeling excited and anxious all at once.

Tina was excited, too. At breakfast she told Dad all about the party. And, although she ate an egg, toast, cereal and orange juice, she didn't stop talking once.

At lunch Tina lunged for the sauce. Then she gobbled down her meal and rushed upstairs to choose her party clothes.

Then Edward heard her, all the way from downstairs.

"Hic-hic! Hic-hic!"

"Oh no!" groaned Edward. "There she goes!"

Mum made Tina drink a glass of water upside down. Then Mum, Tina and Edward walked very gently to the party. Edward kept his paws crossed all the way.

But just as Mum rang the doorbell – "Hic!" – Tina got hiccups again. Edward didn't know where to put himself.

At last the door opened. Edward was almost too embarrassed to go inside. But when he did, Edward couldn't believe his eyes – or his ears!

Because all the bear owners were rushing at their food. They all seemed to be shrieking as they ate. And, to Edward's delight, every single owner had… hiccups!

Whizz Fizz Bear

Nigel liked a night-time nibble. As soon as the house was quiet, he would creep downstairs to explore the fridge.

Nigel's favourite food was cheese. And one day Nigel's owner, Harry, popped something really tasty into the shopping trolley.

"Good heavens, Harry!" cried Dad. "This cheese is *exceptional!*"

Nigel waited impatiently for night-time. At last the house was quiet.

"Mmmm!" murmured Nigel as he sampled the latest flavour. And before he knew it, Nigel's nibble had become a mammoth meal.

Now Nigel was feeling thirsty… *very* thirsty. He delved deeper into the fridge.

"Bother!" grumbled Nigel. "This carton of orange juice is empty." But then he saw the bottle.

Fun Fizz said the cheerful label. And then, in smaller letters, *'guaranteed to quench your thirst'*.

Nigel reached for it eagerly. He'd never managed to open a bottle by himself before. But this time he was in luck – the bottle was half empty, and the cap was loose.

Whizz, Fizz! A million bubbles tickled Nigel's nose.

Whizz, Fizz! Nigel had never tasted *anything* like it!

Very soon the bottle was empty.

But then Nigel noticed the crate. It was parked by the back door, and it was *full* of Fizz.

Nigel skipped across the kitchen. But this time he was out of luck. Because, though he tried every single bottle, he couldn't open any of them.

Reluctantly, Nigel padded back to bed. But he couldn't get the Fizz out of his mind.

Nigel tossed and turned. He'd never been so thirsty. Then, suddenly, he found himself back in the quiet kitchen again. And this time it was a different story.

"Whizz, Fizz, wow!" cried Nigel, as he opened the first bottle with ease. "Being thirsty must have made me stronger!

Whizz, Fizz! Whizz, Fizz! Nigel worked his way steadily through the crate. By the time he reached the last bottle, he was feeling light-headed, light-pawed and…

"Help!" cried Nigel. He was so full of bubbles that he had begun to float – just like a helium balloon!

First Nigel glided through the kitchen. Next he hovered in the hall. Then – *whoosh!* – he floated up the stairs and into Harry's bedroom.

"Oh no!" cried Nigel. "The window's open!"

Nigel was in a panic. He didn't want to fly off into the night. He would be heartbroken to leave his happy home and fridge.

So, with a desperate lunge, Nigel grabbed hold of Harry's bookshelf.

Crash! Down came all Harry's books. And so did Nigel.

Slowly, he opened one eye. But all Nigel could see was the familiar design on Harry's wallpaper.

Gradually, Nigel came to his senses. Then, suddenly, he gave a great "*Whoop!*"

"I didn't drink all the Fizz after all!" cried Nigel. "I've just been having a nightmare, and I've fallen out of bed."

Nigel wriggled with relief. But he was still thirsty. Then he saw the tumbler of water. Harry's dad had left it by the bed, just in case the new cheese had made Harry thirsty. Nigel drank deeply. Then he settled back into bed and a happy, dreamlike sleep.

The next day Harry's family had visitors. Harry and Nigel were on their best behaviour.

And, when the drinks were poured, Nigel shook his head politely at the Fizz.

"No thanks," he seemed to say. "Mine's an orange juice."

The Bear and the Babysitter

The new babysitter was due any minute. And Buster was sulking in Ben's room.

The last babysitter had been bossy and banished them to bed early. The babysitter before that had been fussy. *She'd* scrubbed behind their ears!

And now... *ding, dong!*

Help! Here she is! thought Buster. And he slid smartly into Ben's playhouse.

Buster could hear hello and goodbye noises coming from the hall. Then he heard Ben calling his name.

But, although Buster sat in the playhouse for a long time, there were no getting-ready-for-bed noises. And once or twice he thought he heard squeaks of excitement.

Buster padded softly onto the landing and listened again.

"Oh no!" he groaned. "They're playing my favourite game. And they've started without me!"

Buster squirmed with disappointment.

Then – *Brring! Brring!* – the phone rang in the kitchen.

Whoosh! As soon as the babysitter left the living room, Buster whizzed down the stairs.

"A wrong number," the babysitter explained, coming back into the hall. Then she caught sight of Buster at the bottom of the stairs, looking innocent and interesting.

"Look, Ben!" she cried. "I told you your teddy would turn up. Now he can join in our game."

Buster and Ben went to bed late that evening. There was barely time to wash before their story. And, when she tucked them in, the babysitter smiled kindly.

"The first family I babysat for," she confided, "were a bit bossy. And the next family were fairly fussy. But this must be third time lucky," she said, "because you two are *brilliant!*"

And so are you, thought Buster. *And so are you.*

The Teddy
Who Wanted a T-shirt

Sandy looked in the mirror in disgust.

"Same old velvet waistcoat. Boring old spotty tie," he grumbled.
"I must be the worst-dressed bear in town."

Later that day, Sandy's owner had a visitor. And Tess had brought
her teddy.

When they were introduced, Sandy wriggled in his wretched
waistcoat. He squirmed in his terrible tie. Because the visiting
teddy looked terrific… in a trendy new T-shirt.

That evening Sandy stuffed his tie down the side of
the chair. He turned his waistcoat back to front.

"But it still doesn't look like a T-shirt," he growled.

The next day, Sandy's owner went shopping. He came home with a carrier bag full of new T-shirts.

Mum suddenly got brisk and busy. "We'll pass on all your outgrown T-shirts," she announced. "But first we must give them a wash."

Sandy's owner parked him on the washing machine and ran out to play.

Sandy looked on with longing as Mum loaded in the T-shirts. "Ooooh, look at those lovely stripes!" he sighed.

No sooner had Mum disappeared than Sandy shuffled to the front of the machine. Gingerly, he leaned over the edge to look for the STOP button.

If only I could rescue just one T-shirt, he thought to himself. But everything looked so strange upside down. And, instead of the STOP button, Sandy's nose nudged the EXTRA HOT button.

Later, when Mum unloaded the machine, she squealed in surprise. Because every single T-shirt had been shrunk… to *exactly* Sandy's size!

Midnight in the Park

You know the bear from Number Nine,
She likes to play at night.
Down the drainpipe watch her whizz,
There's not a soul in sight.

She tries a cartwheel on the grass,
She longs to stretch her paws.
Then on the swing she starts to sing,
"It's great to be outdoors!"

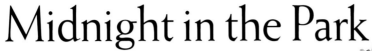

"Psst!" Someone's creeping up the path,
They want to try the slide.
It's Twenty-three and Seven B:
"We couldn't stay inside!"

Now Twenty-two is coming too,
And Seventeen and Four,
They're jumping off the climbing frame,
Then running back for more.

But suddenly a light appears,
"What's going on out there?"
A small boy cries and tries to see,
"And where's my teddy bear?"

Up the drainpipe, home they go,
Before it starts to rain,
They leave the park all still and dark,
But they'll be back again!

Christmas Bear

A tear rolled down Sally's cheek as her mother switched off the bedroom light. It was Christmas Eve, and Sally had forgotten to post her letter to Santa Claus. She had found it stuffed in her jacket pocket.

How would Santa know what Sally really wanted? Maybe he'd forget her altogether!

Sally and her parents had still put out two mince pies and a glass of milk to welcome Santa. The red stocking hung ready at the foot of her bed as it did every Christmas Eve. But this year Sally was sure it would remain empty.

She sniffed miserably to herself as she drifted off to sleep…

Meanwhile, a bright shape was racing through the starry sky. It was Santa Claus, riding in his biggest sleigh, pulled by his fastest reindeer!

The sleigh was filled with sacks of presents, neatly sorted and labelled for children all over the world.

But in one of the sacks something was stirring…

A little paw appeared, and then another. Then two ears, followed by a furry head and a furry body.

It was a teddy bear… a very naughty teddy bear!

The sleigh made a sudden turn. One second the teddy bear was safe inside the sack, and the next he was tumbling down, over and over and over. He gave one shrill squeak, but Santa Claus heard nothing except the rushing of the wind and the jingling of the reindeer's bells.

Over and over Bear fell, towards white fields far below.

Down...

and down...

and down he went...

until suddenly he landed in the snow-laden branches of a fir tree.

"Ouch!" he cried as he slid through the prickly branches and disappeared into a deep snowdrift.

All was still and silent and very, very cold.

Bear couldn't tell whether he was upside down or the right way up. It was some time before he pushed away the snow and found himself looking out into the night.

A little way off he saw a person dressed all in white.

"Aha!" said Bear. "*There's* someone who will help me."

He struggled to his feet and trudged through the snow, which as you can imagine seemed very deep to a little bear.

"Excuse me," he called out as he came closer. "Can you please tell me where I am?"

There was no answer from the person dressed in white.

Bear tried once more. "Excuse me," he said loudly. "Can you tell me where I am?"

Again there was no answer. The person in white didn't even look down to see who was talking.

"Well!" said Bear, turning away. "I hope all the people here aren't so rude!"

95

Bear was now feeling very cold and sorry for himself. He wished he was safe and snug in Santa's sack.

He sighed and looked around. Not far off there was a house. *And where there is a house,* Bear thought to himself, *there will be people and warmth.*

He walked round the house twice, trying to find a way in, but the door handles and windows were all too high for him to reach.

He was about to give up when a black cat came padding round the corner. It stopped and looked the little bear up and down, its fur bristling and its whiskers twitching. Then, deciding that bears were of no great interest, the cat turned and walked away.

The cat climbed up some steps to a closed door and then vanished completely. The last Bear saw of it was its tail disappearing through the unopened door.

A magic cat! thought Bear.

But he soon discovered that the cat had its own private cat-sized door. There in front of him was a hinged flap.

Bear reached up and pushed himself against it. The next thing he knew, he was tumbling head-first through the opening.

Bear thumped down onto a soft carpet. What bliss to be inside!

For a minute he lay still with his eyes shut, enjoying the warmth and comfort. Then he opened his eyes.

It was very dark. In front of him there was a staircase, and at the top he saw a dim light.

It's time for a good snooze, Bear thought. He'd had enough adventures for a while.

Bear dragged himself up towards the light. He was out of breath when he pulled himself up the last step.

The light was coming from an open door. From inside, Bear could hear the sound of soft breathing.

He tiptoed to the door and nearly tripped over something lying just inside. It was a plate with two mince pies on it! Next to it was a small glass of milk.

Now, Bear felt very hungry indeed. He sat himself down by the plate and ate steadily and happily until he had finished both pies.

How kind of them to think of me! Bear thought, gulping down the milk.

It was only then that he started to look around the room. In one corner there was a bed, and in it someone was sleeping peacefully.

"That's where I'd like to be," Bear whispered.

It wasn't easy getting up onto the bed, but he finally did it. A tired bear can be a very determined bear if he spots a comfortable place to sleep.

The effort was worth it. For what should he find at the end of the bed but a cosy red sleeping bag. It was just the right size!

In no time at all, he snuggled his way into it and fell fast asleep...

Sally opened her eyes. It was morning. *Christmas* morning!

But Sally's heart sank as she remembered her unposted letter to Santa.

Had he brought her anything at all? She looked towards the door. The mince pies and the milk had gone!

Quickly she crawled down to the bottom of the bed. The red stocking was no longer flat and empty. It was bulging. There really *was* something in it!

Bursting with excitement, she reached in and pulled out… a furry teddy bear!

Sally gazed at it wide-eyed. "But how could Santa have known you were exactly what I wanted?" she asked the little bear, thinking of the letter in her jacket pocket. This is what it said:

Dear Santa,
    Please can I have my very own bear for Christmas?

    Lots of love
    Sally
    x x x

Was it Sally's imagination, or did the little bear seem to smile?

ANIMAL STORIES

About the stories...

Animals are very special friends for children. In a child's imagination they can play, walk, talk, have fun, and enjoy the most amazing adventures. The twenty stories and seven rhymes that follow feature all sorts of animal friends—a duck who doesn't like the rain, a clumsy bunny rabbit, a kitten who is afraid of the dark, a clever young dragon—and a crocodile who likes to dance and climb trees.

Contents

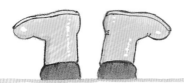

New Boots for Rabbit

One morning Rabbit looked outside and saw that it was raining. He remembered his new boots, and he hurried to put them on.

"It's raining out," said Rabbit to his mother. "Let's go for a walk so I can wear my new boots."

But Rabbit's mother was busy, and she said, "In a little while, Rabbit, when I finish my work."

So Rabbit began to play on his own, with his new boots on.

"With these boots," he whispered, "I could walk into a river and catch the biggest fish in the whole world." And he pretended he was a fisherman pulling in a huge fish.

Then Rabbit said to his mother, "Is it time to go for a walk now?"

"Later," replied his mother, because she was still busy.

So Rabbit played on his own some more.

"With these boots," he said, "I could be a sailor in a storm, travelling all over the world." And he pretended he was in a boat, tossing on the sea.

When he had finished playing, he called to his mother, "Are you ready yet?"

"Not quite," answered his mother.

One more time Rabbit went off to play.

"With these boots," he said, "I could be an explorer in the jungle." And he imagined himself walking through a rain forest, discovering birds and animals.

At last Rabbit heard his mother say, "Time to go now!" So, together, they went out for a walk.

But what a surprise! The rain had stopped, and the sun was drying up the puddles. Rabbit was so disappointed and cross that he felt like crying. He had waited all that time to get his new boots wet, and now the sun was shining!

Rabbit and his mother kept walking until they reached the park. Rabbit began to feel a bit better. He and his mother could look at the fountain with the little pool all around it, and that was always fun.

Suddenly someone shouted, "Oh, dear me, help!"

It was an elegant lady in smart clothes, and her hat had blown into the fountain.

"I'll get it!" said Rabbit, and quickly he waded into the little pool to rescue the hat.

"Oh, thank you," said the elegant lady when Rabbit returned the hat. "How lucky that you were wearing your boots." She smiled at Rabbit. "With boots like those, maybe someday you'll be a fisherman, or a sailor, or even an explorer!"

On the way home Rabbit felt very pleased and proud, and he skipped along in his new, wet boots. "With boots like these," he thought, "who knows *what* might happen?"

The Duck Who Didn't Like Rain

Derek was a new duckling. He lived with his family by the Big Pond.

Mr and Mrs Duck were proud of their ducklings. Every morning they took them for a long walk.

It was a long, dry spring that year. But at last it rained. And that's when the trouble started.

Mrs Duck was excited to see the rain. She lifted her wing carefully and woke the ducklings. "Look, children," she said. "It's a lovely wet day!"

The ducklings rubbed the sleep from their eyes. "Is that the rain you told us about, Mum?" they asked, beeping with excitement.

"Yes, indeed," she said. "Now hurry and line up. Your father's ready to go!"

"Let us proceed!" cried Mr Duck, and the Duck family set off in a long line. But Derek lagged behind.

"What is it, dear?" asked his mother gently.

"Don't like it," said Derek in a small voice. "Don't like the rain. Makes my toes feel tickly."

"Makes your *toes* feel tickly?" cried Derek's father. "Whoever heard of a duckling with tickly toes?"

Mrs Duck didn't shout. That evening she paid a visit to Old Ma Goat. Ma Goat kept a shop, and she sold almost everything you could think of.

Mrs Duck was in luck. Ma Goat had some wellingtons, just the right size for Derek.

Next time it rained, Mrs Duck gave Derek the wellingtons.

"Let us depart!" cried Mr Duck.

"How's that, Derek?" asked Mrs Duck gently.

"Still don't like it," whispered Derek. "Musses up my feathers. Spoils my hair."

"Spoils your *hair*?" cried Derek's father. He was very upset to have a child who worried about his hair.

115

Mrs Duck went back to Old Ma Goat. What luck! Ma Goat had a smart cape and hood, just the right size for Derek.

Next time it rained, the Duck family shouted cheerfully, "Hurry up, Derek. Put on your cape and wellingtons."

"How's that, dear?" asked Mrs Duck.

"It's *lovely*, Mum," replied Derek.

Suddenly he saw a huge rainbow. "What's *that*?" he asked.

"That, my boy," said his father, "is a rainbow. A rainbow comes when the sun tries to shine through the rain."

"It's beautiful!" said Derek, gazing up at the bright colours. Then he looked around in wonder. Everything sparkled in the rain!

After that, Derek wanted it to rain every day. He didn't always see a rainbow. But he loved exploring in the rain. And sometimes he was in such a hurry to get started that he even forgot to put on his cape and wellingtons!

Mervyn's Glasses

It was dawn. Like all night birds, Mr and Mrs Owl were preparing for bed.

"I'm worried about Mervyn," said Mrs Owl. "I don't think he sees well."

"You worry too much, my dear," said Mr Owl, snuggling up to his wife. "Mervyn's just fine. Now you get a good day's sleep."

The Owl family slept all day. At dusk they woke up, and Mr Owl flew off to work.

All that night, Mrs Owl watched Mervyn carefully. She was right. Mervyn *couldn't* see well. He didn't always empty his plate. He held his new book too close to his eyes.

At bedtime Mrs Owl spoke to her husband again. "Tomorrow," she told him, "we must take Mervyn straight to Mr Specs. He'll soon put Mervyn right."

When Mervyn woke up, Mrs Owl explained the plan.

"But I don't want to wear glasses," said Mervyn. "They'll fall down my beak. They'll make me look silly."

"You'll look very handsome," Mrs Owl assured him. "Your father wears glasses, and there's nothing wrong with *his* looks!"

Mervyn enjoyed the visit to Mr Specs. Mr Specs tested his eyes with all kinds of charts and lenses. And Mervyn enjoyed choosing the frames for his glasses—it was fun seeing all the different shapes and colours they came in.

A week later, Mervyn and his mum went back to collect his glasses. Mr Specs held up a big mirror, and Mervyn saw himself clearly for the first time.

"What a fine bird I am!" he thought. "But I *don't* like my glasses!"

On the way home, Mervyn noticed all kinds of new things.

"Look at the stars!" he shouted. "And see those glow worms! These glasses work a treat."

But when he got home, Mervyn caught sight of himself in the mirror. "Silly old glasses!" he said to himself, stamping up and down his branch, crossly.

Just then the postman arrived. "Special delivery,"
he said, handing Mervyn a letter.

"What lovely big writing," said Mervyn. "It's an invitation," he
told his parents, "to David's party. But I'm not going... *not in these
glasses!*"

All week Mr and Mrs Owl tried to persuade Mervyn to change
his mind. "Please go to the party," they said. "All your friends will
be there. You don't want to disappoint David, do you?"

On the night of the party, Mervyn's dad tried one last time.

Mervyn shook his head.

"Well," said Dad, "if you don't want to play games and win prizes
and eat a party tea, that's up to you. I only wish I could go!"

Mervyn started to think about all the other owls having fun. He
thought about the sandwiches and lemonade and cake and ice
cream. And in the end he decided to go to the party. He wrapped
David's present and brushed his feathers. Then he flew there, all
by himself.

David was waiting on his branch to greet Mervyn.

Mervyn landed gracefully and held out the present.
And when he looked up at
David, he got a super surprise.

David was wearing glasses,
too. And he looked
so handsome!

121

The Dirty Dinosaur

"Just look at your knees, Douglas!" cried Mrs Dinosaur.

"*Brrm, brrm,*" said Douglas. He was much too busy with his car to look at his knees.

"Have you seen your face, Douglas?" asked Mr Dinosaur.

"*Brrm, brrm,*" said Douglas. He was much too busy driving his car to look in the mirror.

"Don't you ever take a bath?" sighed Granny Dinosaur.

"*Brrm, brrm,*" said Douglas. He *never* had time for a bath!

One day the Dinosaurs went to town. On their way, they passed a sign. CAR WASH, it said, in big letters.

"Brrm, brrm!" said Douglas. And before you could say "diplodocus," he was inside.

"Douglas, come out of there!" cried Mum, Dad and Granny Dinosaur.

But Douglas was having too much fun! "Ooooh!" he cried. "It tickles… but I like it!"

At last Douglas came out of the car wash. "That was lovely!" he said. And for the first time ever, Douglas was clean… all over!

The Rainbow Rabbits

"Who's got my socks?" cried Mr Rabbit one morning. "Just wait until I find out which one of you naughty little bunnies has got them. Now then, Bayleaf – show me your feet!"

But the little rabbit just giggled. "I'm not Bayleaf, Dad," he said innocently. "I'm Bluebell. And these aren't *your* socks, they're Hazel's. And Hazel is wearing Scarlet's socks. And Scarlet is wearing Snowdrop's socks. And Rosebud isn't wearing any socks at all. And…"

"Stop!" cried Mr Rabbit. "You're making my ears spin!" He peered closely at the little bunny in front of him. "Are you *sure* you're not Bayleaf? No? Well, never mind. The point is that everything is in a muddle. No one knows who's wearing what, and I still haven't found my socks! There's only one answer to a mess like this – we need a *system*!"

Mrs Rabbit sighed. She remembered her husband's "Patent Improved Carrot-Cooking System" – the steam had peeled off all the wallpaper. And as for his "Water-Saving Ear-Washing System" – her ears had lost their wiggle for *weeks*!

Before long the floor was tail-deep in paper. "Don't stand on those charts!" cried Mr Rabbit, waving his crayons. "Now, everybody stand still and listen. My new system is based on *colour co-ordination*! And," he added modestly, "it's brilliant! What do you think?" he asked his wife.

"It's brilliant," said Mrs Rabbit, faintly.

In a few days Mr Rabbit's system was in operation. Little Scarlet was dressed from paws to ears all in red. Primrose was all in yellow. You can guess what happened to Bayleaf, Snowdrop, Hazel, Bluebell and Rosebud!

At first the seven little bunnies rather liked looking different from one another. But pretty soon they started to complain.

"I don't *like* brown," said Hazel. "I want a T-shirt like Bluebell's!"

"I'm never going to get dressed again if I have to wear horrible *green!*" wailed Bayleaf.

Mrs Rabbit could hardly think straight with all the complaining. But Mr Rabbit insisted that, with a few minor adjustments, everything would be fine.

He set to work again with his famous crayons. But at the end of the day, he accidentally left the crayons in his shirt pocket and then put the shirt in the washing machine with all the children's clothes.

When Mrs Rabbit took the washing out of the machine next morning, she laughed so loudly that the little rabbits came running. "What's the matter, Mum?" they asked.

Mrs Rabbit choked and sniffled. "I don't want to hear one more word about... ho ho ho... your clothes," she giggled. "Your father has... hee hee hee... invented a new system called... ha ha ha... the *Improved* Colour Co-ordination System – and we're *all* going to be using it!"

The little rabbits loved their multicoloured clothes.

"Well, it *was* time for... hh-hmm!... Phase Two of my System," said Mr Rabbit, looking aimlessly at the ceiling.

The Kitten
and the Kangaroo

The kitten and the kangaroo
Were bored and wondered what to do.
"I know," said Kanga, "take a ride!
Here's my pouch – just hop inside."

The kitten took a mighty leap.
"I say," she said, "you're mighty steep!"
"Come on," said Kanga, "grab a paw,
I'll take you on a guided tour."

The twosome bounced across the town.
"Gee-up!" said Kitten. "Don't slow down!"
But Kanga groaned, "I've had enough.
I'm high on bounce and low on puff."

"But I've no pouch," the kitten cried,
"To give my weary friend a ride."
She thought and sighed and thought some more,
Then rushed off to the superstore.

The boss was kind. He heard her plan.
"I'd like to help you if I can.
Here's a trolley – take good care –
I think your friend could fit in there."

So Kanga rode back home in style,
While Kitten pushed and gave a smile.
"I may be small, but you will find
I'll *never* leave a friend behind!"

An Up and Down Story

Mrs Kangaroo was on top of the world. She had a brand new baby. The baby was called Clifford.

Mrs Kangaroo rang up her friend. "Come and see my son," she said.

The friend hopped over right away. She brought a big book on child care. "I can give you some tips as well," she said. "With three children of my own, I know a thing or two."

Mrs Kangaroo listened to her friend's advice. She read the book carefully. More than anything, she wanted to be a good mother.

Clifford settled down quickly. He slept through the night. He gurgled through the day.

"Being a mum is easy," thought Mrs Kangaroo.
"It's time to get out and about." She telephoned her
friend. "We'll hop over for coffee," she said.

Mrs Kangaroo dressed Clifford in his best clothes and popped
him into her pouch. Then she set off at top speed.

But before she got to the end of the road, Clifford started wailing.
He'd never made such a dreadful noise before. Whatever could be
the matter?

Mrs Kangaroo lifted Clifford out of her pouch and looked at him.
She remembered everything she had read in her book, and she
checked Clifford carefully. But he was clean and dry. He didn't
have wind. She knew he couldn't be hungry, because she had just
fed him.

Then Mrs Kangaroo noticed Clifford's face. It wasn't kangaroo-
coloured at all. Clifford's face was a most awful shade of green!

Mrs Kangaroo was alarmed. Clifford must have the horrible
disease the book had mentioned. It was called 'travel sickness',
and it affected very young kangaroos who weren't used to their
mother's hopping yet.

Sadly Mrs Kangaroo tiptoed the rest of
the way to her friend's house. She went
as smoothly as she could, but it's
difficult for a kangaroo not
to hop at all.

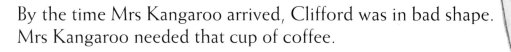

By the time Mrs Kangaroo arrived, Clifford was in bad shape. Mrs Kangaroo needed that cup of coffee.

"It's nothing to worry about," said her friend. "Just get some Bouncewell medicine for him."

Mrs Kangaroo went straight to the chemist's and bought some. "Put a teaspoonful in Clifford's next bottle," advised the chemist.

After Clifford's feed, Mrs Kangaroo set off hopefully for the shops. But the medicine didn't work. Clifford wailed all afternoon.

When she got home, Mrs Kangaroo rang her friend. "That medicine you told me about is no good," she complained. "Clifford's all green again, and I don't know *what* to do!"

"Don't worry," said her friend. "Lots of baby kangaroos get travel sickness. Clifford will soon grow out of it."

But Mrs Kangaroo couldn't wait for Clifford to grow out of it. She didn't want to be stuck at home all day. Being a mum wasn't so easy after all. Someone should have warned her.

That afternoon, while she was tidying the hall cupboard, Mrs Kangaroo found her old roller skates. As she looked at them, she began to get very excited. Could these be the answer to Clifford's problem?

The next day Mrs Kangaroo took Clifford for a trial run. She crossed her fingers for luck, because she didn't know *what* was going to happen.

Wheeee... Mrs Kangaroo set off down the street. She soon got the hang of her skates again. Clifford had never had such a smooth ride.

In no time at all Mrs Kangaroo was halfway across town. Clifford's face was still a beautiful kangaroo colour, and Mum wasn't stuck at home.

But Mrs Kangaroo was careful not to skate past the police station. She would hate to get arrested for speeding!

Slippy and the Skaters

There was once a bunny called Cowslip who was very clumsy. She bumped into furniture; she dropped her toast on the floor – jam side down – and she tripped over her own feet.

When Cowslip poured herself a drink, her mum would say, "Give that to me, Slippy. I'll carry it into the dining room. We don't want *more* milk in the pot plants, do we?"

Cowslip didn't mean to be careless. It was just that she didn't think about what she was doing. Her mind was always on something else.

At playgroup the little bunnies ran round the room to music.

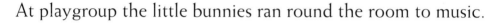

Hoppity, skippety, JUMP!
Hoppity, skippety, JUMP!
Hoppity, skippety, BUMP!

Yes, that was Cowslip. She'd noticed a spider high up on the ceiling and had forgotten to jump.

It seemed that hardly a day went by without Cowslip colliding with one of her friends or spilling her food – or without someone telling her to concentrate and *think* about what she was doing.

One winter the water in the village pond froze so hard that it was safe to skate on. All the little bunnies, and some of the big ones as well, whizzed and swooped across the ice. Cowslip went along too, and started to put on her skates.

"Oh Slippy, *please* don't come on the ice," shouted her brother. "You're sure to knock everyone over!"

"Perhaps you'd better just sit quietly on the bank and think, Slippy," advised her mum, who was practising her famous double-axel bunny-loop.

135

So Cowslip sat down on the bank and enjoyed watching her mum. She was a brilliant skater.

Soon the little bunny's mind moved on to other things. She noticed the way the ducks slithered and slipped on the ice, and wondered why they didn't wear skates. She noticed that old Bunny Hopkins was wearing odd socks and that his jacket didn't quite fit. She noticed that the ice was melting in the middle of the pond… *WHAT?*

"*STOP!*" cried Cowslip. "The ice is melting!"

In only a minute or two all the skaters were safely off the ice. Now they could see the growing hole in the middle, too.

"Well done, Slippy," said her mum. "You were the only one thinking about the really important things. If not for you, my double-axel bunny-loop—and your brothers and sisters—might never have been seen again!"

Chickens

We are the chickens,
(In case you hadn't guessed!)
We are the chickens,
We think you'll be impressed!

We slide down the haystack,
We balance on the coop,
We fly in strict formation
And *always* loop the loop!

We dive from the dovecote,
We stagger to a stop.
We like to chase the sheep,
And then to ride on top!

We bounce on the tractor,
We give the horn a *beep*!
We gallop round the yard,
And *never* go to sleep!

We are the chickens!
Our farmer needs a rest.
But still he tells his friends,
"MY CHICKENS ARE THE BEST!"

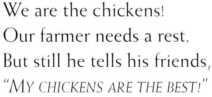

Brown Bear's Visit

Brown Bear had just finished breakfast. "That was horrible," he grumbled. "What's next?"

"Next," said Mum, "you can go to the playground while I tidy up."

At the playground, Brown Bear began to grizzle. "Same old friends, same old slide. It wouldn't be so bad if we had a climbing frame here!"

Brown Bear was grouchy all day. Then, when he got home, Mum sent him off to the waterfall for a shower.

"I hate getting clean!" he moaned. "Why can't I stay dirty sometimes?"

Brown Bear grumbled as he gobbled his supper. He grizzled as he snuggled into bed. Mum tucked him in and told him a story.

"That was boring," he yawned. Then he turned over and fell asleep.

Next morning Brown Bear had a visitor.
It was his cousin Billy Bear from
across the mountain.

"Can you come to play?" Billy
Bear asked. "Mum says you
can stay the night."

Brown Bear was so keen to go he
barely said goodbye to his mum. He didn't even wave to his
friends on the slide. He just jogged along beside his cousin and
asked what they were going to do first.

"First," said Billy Bear, "we'll go to the playground so I can show
you our climbing frame. Then I'll take you home to meet
the twins."

Brown Bear couldn't wait to try
the climbing frame. "It's easy,"
said Billy. "Just watch me and my
friends!" And they clambered up
to the top of the climbing frame
and began swinging from the
highest bars.

Brown Bear tried to do the same.
But he had never climbed so
high before. He fell off and
bumped his nose!

Billy didn't seem to notice.
He carried on climbing and
swinging with his friends until it
was time to go home.

As they neared home, Brown Bear smelt something cooking. The thought of food cheered him up. But Auntie was behind schedule.

"It's those twins," she explained. "They're always under my feet!"

But then she had a brainwave. "Why don't you big bears take the little ones to the river? You can bath them for me. And bath yourselves at the same time."

"I don't like rivers," said Brown Bear. "Why can't we go to the waterfall?"

"Because we don't have one," said Auntie simply, as she began to tidy up.

As soon as they reached the river, the twins squirted Brown Bear and Billy. Then, just when it was time to go home, they rolled on the bank and got all dirty again—and splashed mud all over Brown Bear and Billy. Brown Bear had *never* been so cross—or so hungry!

141

142

"Here you are at last," said Auntie, when they finally got home. But as soon as she brought in supper, the other bears swooped down like vultures. There was hardly anything at all left for Brown Bear.

Brown Bear's tummy was still rumbling when he went to bed. It was so dark he couldn't even see his cousins.

"Can I have a story?" he called out.

But Auntie was already snoring. And so were all the other bears.

The next day Billy led Brown Bear along the track. He pointed in the direction of Brown Bear's home. "Look," he said. "Your mum's coming to meet you."

Brown Bear barely said goodbye to his cousin. He bounded along the track as fast as his legs would carry him.

"It *is* good to see you, Brown Bear," said Mum. "Now, what would you like to do first?"

Brown Bear nestled up to Mum. He put his nose in the air and breathed in the sweet smells of home.

"Lovely friends! Lovely slide! Lovely waterfall! Lovely meals! Lovely stories!" he cried. "And I want to do it *all* first!"

The Puppy Who Went Exploring

Prudence the puppy was very excited. It had been such a thrilling day! She had started it living in one place, and now she was living somewhere completely different.

Her family had moved into a new house. Prudence couldn't wait to go exploring, even though she'd be going on her own. Her mum and dad and sister all said they had too much to do.

"See you later, everybody," she said, and trotted off.

"Don't get into any mischief, now," her dad called.

"Really," thought Prudence, "as if I would!"

Prudence went through the nearest door, and found herself approaching a cave full of interesting things. She snuffled inside it for a while, but then the things attacked her.

"Yikes!" said Prudence. "I'm off!"

She skidded into a nearby room, where she saw a strange box thing standing in the corner. She stood on her hind legs and sniffed at it… and suddenly it made a very loud noise!

"Yikes!" said Prudence. "I'm off!"

She scampered up the stairs and dashed into another room. There she found a big, puffy thing that was just right for biting and tugging… but it tried to smother her!

"Yikes!" said Prudence. "I'm off!"

She shot across the landing, rolled down the stairs, and landed at the bottom with a *bump*! And that's where the rest of the family found her when they came running.

"Prudence!" said her mum. "What *do* you think you're up to?"

"Quick, everybody," said Prudence breathlessly. "Let's get out of here before it's too late…"

When they'd stopped laughing, Prudence's family showed her round the house. She discovered that the cave was a broom cupboard, the box thing was a television, and the puffy thing a duvet. To make her feel more cheerful, Prudence's dad found her a bone. And next time she went exploring — she didn't go alone!

The Trouble With Babies

One day Timmy's mum sat him on her knee. "Timmy," she said, "soon you are going to have some little brothers and sisters to play with. Won't that be nice?"

Timmy was very excited. He was tired of playing all by himself and he could hardly wait for the new bunnies to be born. He tidied up his toy box and started to think of good games he could play with his brothers and sisters.

He lined up all his cars and his big yellow tractor under the table. "This can be Timmy's Garage," he thought. "The little bunnies can drive my cars, and I will be Chief Mechanic."

"Come and see your new brothers and sisters!" said Timmy's dad a few days later. Mum was sitting up in bed holding four little bundles. Timmy tiptoed forward.

"But they're tiny!" he squeaked in surprise. They certainly didn't look big enough to drive his big yellow tractor.

"They'll grow very fast," laughed Mum.

But the babies didn't grow very fast at all. They were still tiny the next day, and the day after that. They seemed to be asleep nearly all the time – and they wouldn't even open their eyes!

A few weeks later the little bunnies started to smile and gurgle. Timmy waited until his mum was out of the room.

"It's all right," he whispered to his brothers and sisters. "She's not here. You can stop pretending now and talk to me." But the little bunnies just smiled and gurgled some more.

"Come and see my garage," said Timmy. But the little bunnies didn't seem at all interested.

Mum found Timmy looking sad. "My new brothers and sisters don't like me," he said. "They won't talk to me, and they don't want to share my toys."

"But Timmy," said his mum, "that's because they're only a few weeks old, and you are a big bunny now. They have a lot to learn, and *you* can help me teach them to do all the things that you can do."

So Timmy put away his cars and his big yellow tractor. "Little bunnies are not ready to play with big toys yet," he announced. "They have a lot to learn."

Then he piled some cushions and his picture books under the table. "This is Timmy's School," he said. "And I am the Baby Bunny Teacher!"

Mrs Bunny Had Twins

What wonderful news!
But what names would she choose?
So many relatives
Had their own views.

Said old Uncle Boris,
"Have you thought of Horace?
And Doris? Or Morris?
Or Norris? Or... *Boris?*"

Smiled Grandmother Connie,
"Dear, what about Ronnie?
And Bonnie? Or Jonnie?
Or Lonnie? Or... *Connie?*"

Cried young Cousin Harry,
"But what about Barry?
And Carrie? Or Larry?
Or Gary? Or... *Harry?*"

Laughed poor Mrs Bunny,
"Here's Sonny. Here's Honey.
For names don't sound funny,
When they rhyme with... *Bunny!*"

The Roly Poly Kitten

Once upon a time there was a Roly Poly Kitten. He was friendly, he was cheerful and, although he didn't know it, he was just a little plump.

One day it rained so hard that the Roly Poly Kitten had to stay indoors. All morning he chased his brothers and sisters.

At last lunchtime came. "Now, sit down," said Dad, "and please eat nicely."

The Roly Poly Kitten bounced up to his place and tucked in. But the other kittens grumbled at him.

"Move over," cried one. "You're taking up all the room!"

"Hey!" squealed another. "You're sitting on my tail!"

But the smallest kitten yelled loudest of all. "Go away!" she cried. "You're a FAT KITTEN, and I can't reach the food!"

Whooooosh! The Roly Poly Kitten ran right out of the house and down the lane, where he hid under a hedge. "I'm fat! I'm fat!" he sniffed. "And nobody likes me." Then he took a deep breath and tried to look thinner – but that only gave him hiccups.

Back home, Dad was worried. "We shall have to make a search party," he announced.

"Oooh, I LOVE parties!" squealed the smallest kitten.

But Dad looked stern. "What I mean," he explained, "is that we must find your brother."

So the kittens went outside to search, and eventually they reached the hedge where the Roly Poly Kitten was hiding. A stranger happened to be walking by.

"I'm looking for my son," Dad told her. "Perhaps you've seen him. Let me describe him for you."

"Oh no!" thought the Roly Poly Kitten. He didn't want to hear how fat he was. But his family shouted so loudly that he *had* to listen.

"He's friendly!"

"He's cheerful!"

"He's handsome!"

"He's strong!"

"He's…" the smallest kitten thought carefully, "he's CUDDLY!"

"That's right," smiled Dad. "He's a very special kitten indeed."

The Roly Poly Kitten was too surprised to speak.

The stranger said she was very sorry, but she hadn't seen him. "Goodness me," sighed Dad. "Wherever can he be?" In the end he and the other kittens went to look at home.

Inside the house, all was still and quiet. But not for long.

Whoooosh! The Roly Poly Kitten sprang out of his hiding place "I feel friendly!" he announced, bounding through the door. "I feel cheerful! I feel handsome! I feel strong! I feel cuddly! But most of all," he cried as he sat down at the table, "I feel… HUNGRY!"

Teamwork

Two leopards were wearing
    A terrible frown.
They wriggled and jiggled
    And jumped up and down.

They twisted, insisted,
    "I *can* count my spots."
Then tumbled and grumbled,
    "I'm tied up in knots!"

They growled and they scowled,
    They hadn't a clue.
Then, all of a sudden,
    They knew what to do.

They bounced and announced,
    As they shook their great paws,
"You can count *my* spots…
    And I will count *yours!*"

Flop Learns to Swim

Flop, the penguin, was nervous. It was time for his first swimming lesson.

"Hurry up!" called Dad at the top of his voice. "We don't want to be late."

"Hey! What about breakfast?" cried Flop. He was hoping he could distract Dad, and then maybe he would forget about swimming.

But Dad just said, "No breakfast till after swimming. Swimming on a full stomach will give you cramp."

Down by the sea Flop got cold feet. He tugged at Dad's flipper. "The water's *f-f-f-freezing!*" he said. "Let's go home for breakfast."

Dad took no notice. "The first thing to learn about swimming," he began, "is to relax."

But Flop didn't feel relaxed. He felt cold and wobbly. "What if I can't do it, Dad?" he whispered. "Everyone will laugh."

Just then a group of young penguins rushed past him. "Watch this, Flop!" they cried.

One by one, the penguins dived into the sea – *splish, splash, splosh* – covering Flop with spray.

154

"Brrrrrr! Brrrrrr!" Flop's beak began to chatter. "Please, Dad," he said, "I want to go home."

But Dad was beginning to enjoy himself. "Never mind them," he said. "Watch *me!*"

Flop shivered miserably on the shore and watched as Dad began his demonstration.

"Deep, *splish*, breaths, *splosh*," Dad gasped. "Chin, *splish*, up, *splosh*," he called. "Now *you* try, Flop!"

Flop took a deep breath and waded towards Dad. But he tripped and fell beak-first into the water.

"HELP! HELP!" yelled Flop. "I'M DROWNING!"

Dad scooped Flop out of the water. He patted him firmly on the back.

Flop choked and spluttered. "I don't want to do any more swimming today," he whispered.

Now it was Dad's turn to choke and splutter. "Call *that* swimming?" he bellowed. "For heaven's sake, Flop, please try and concentrate!"

Flop tried harder and harder to swim. Dad tried harder and harder to teach him. But the harder Dad tried, the louder he shouted.

"Please, Dad," said Flop. "I'm not *deaf*. I just can't swim."

Dad gave a huge sigh and one last demonstration. But it was no use. Flop just couldn't do it.

Dad waddled back to the shore. He sat down with a plop – the picture of disappointment.

Just at that moment, another father arrived in the bay. His young daughter was swimming strongly beside him.

Flop's dad groaned and put his head in his flippers.

Flop felt so sorry for his father that he did a very brave thing. He bobbed carefully out to sea until the water reached right up to his beak. Then he swam along… with one foot on the bottom.

"Look at me! Look at me!" quavered Flop.

"WELL DONE, FLOP!" cried Dad, beaming. He started to strut proudly along the shore.

"Well done!" said the other dad. Then he took a closer look at Flop's father.

"Why, it's old Shortie!" he boomed. "I haven't seen you since those *terrible* swimming lessons. Don't you remember? Our fathers nearly deafened us. In the end we went along with one foot on the bottom – just to keep them happy!"

"*Ahem! Ahem! Ahem!*" For some strange reason Flop's dad couldn't stop coughing.

Flop was fascinated. Fancy that penguin calling his dad "Shortie". And fancy Dad swimming along with *his* foot on the bottom!

Flop began to feel more relaxed. He wriggled his toes in the water and gave a little chortle. Then, all of a sudden, he gave a great *whoop* of delight.

"I'M SWIMMING! I'M SWIMMING!" he cried. And, as he shouted, Flop flipped onto his back and waved both feet in the air… just to prove it!

Dance of the Dolphins

Slow, slow, quick quick, slow,
Ride the waves,
And here we go.

Quick, quick, leap up high,
Arch your back,
It's time to fly!

Fly, fly, puff and blow,
Blow some bubbles
In a row.

Puff, puff, waltz and spin,
Shake your tail,
Flick your fin.

Slow, slow, quick quick, slow,
Take a partner,
Dive down low.

Quick, quick, slow slow, quick,
Listen carefully,
That's the trick!

Cry Bunny
and Scaredy Cat

There was once a timid little rabbit named Daisy, and she cried a lot. *Boo-hoo*, all day long, because she was so frightened and so terribly shy.

"If only I had a friend," she used to say, "things would be different."

But no one wanted to be Daisy's friend, because she cried so much. They teased her instead, and called her a Cry Bunny.

> *"Cry Bunny, Shy Bunny,*
> *Go away!*
> *Cry Bunny, Shy Bunny,*
> *You can't play!"*

They all laughed together as Daisy wandered off alone, looking for something to do by herself.

One day Daisy stood behind a tree watching the others have fun. She saw them skipping and climbing and bouncing balls. They were laughing and calling out to one another as they ran and played. They were having a good time, but Daisy was feeling unhappy, as usual.

Then Daisy heard something that sounded familiar. Teasing voices were shouting,

> "Scaredy Cat, Scaredy Cat,
> Go away!
> Scaredy Cat, Scaredy Cat,
> You can't play!"

Everyone was pointing at Roger Cat. He was walking away with his head down, brushing tears from his eyes.

"How can they be so mean?" thought Daisy. She forgot all about being shy, and hurried over to Roger and smiled at him.

"I'll be your friend," she said. "I'll play with you."

Roger looked up. "Oh thank you, Daisy!" he said. "I'll be your friend, too."

So off they went, Daisy and Roger, far from the others.

Next morning Daisy and Roger walked to the stream. First they had a game of tag on the grassy bank. Then they went fishing and caught a little silver trout.

Next day Roger and Daisy played together again, and the day after that. They found all sorts of good things to do together. One day they played school. Another day they pretended to be pirates on the high seas. They became best friends, and never even thought about crying or being scared.

One afternoon while they were playing in the wood, heavy rain clouds filled the sky. Suddenly Daisy and Roger were caught in a downpour.

As they were hurrying home, they heard a small voice crying, "Help! Help!"

It was hard to see in the heavy rain, but Daisy finally spotted Stanley Squirrel's baby brother stuck in the branch of a tree.

"Don't be afraid!" called Daisy. "We'll get you out!"

The tree was too wet and slippery to climb, so Daisy stood on Roger's shoulders. She reached up and pulled the little squirrel out of the branch. Then, holding him carefully, she slid to the ground and carried him home.

"Oh Daisy," said Mrs Squirrel when she heard what had happened, "how brave of you and Roger!"

She gave her little son a hug, dried him off, and then made Daisy and Roger a cup of cocoa.

Before long everyone had heard about Daisy and Roger's daring rescue.

"I suppose Daisy isn't a Cry Bunny any more," said Rosie Fox.

"And Roger isn't a Scaredy Cat after all," said Stanley Squirrel.

"I hope they can play with us tomorrow," said Bonnie Badger.

So Daisy and Roger, who used to get teased for being frightened and shy, turned out to be quite brave and bold after all. And soon they had lots of friends.

Best of all, nobody ever called them Cry Bunny or Scaredy Cat again.

164

The Dancing Bunny

Do you know young Hoppy
Who never can keep still?
If you haven't seen him,
Then you certainly will.

He jigs in the sunshine,
He hops in the drizzle,
He zooms out of the house
With a double-toed twizzle.

From breakfast to supper
He dances and jiggles,
He waggles and waltzes,
He prances and wiggles.

And when sleepy Hoppy
Is tucked up in bed,
He's dancing the fox-trot
Inside his own head!

The Runaway Mouse

"I'm just popping out for some supper," said Mrs Mouse.

A few minutes later, she staggered back with a huge hunk of cheese.

"Ooooh!" squeaked five small voices. "Please can we have some now, Mum?"

"No," said Mrs Mouse. "This cheese is for supper."

But the smallest mouse couldn't wait. When no one was looking, she took a big, big bite.

Mmmmmm! The cheese tasted wonderful! So she took another bite, and another… until Mum caught her.

"Bed!" cried Mrs Mouse. "And no more cheese for a week!"

The little mouse felt so sorry for herself that she bolted right out of their hole and into the big wide farmyard.

"Watch out!" cried a cross voice. It belonged to a puppy.

"I'm running away," the little mouse told him. "Mum shouted at me. She said I couldn't have any more cheese."

"But did she stop you playing football?" asked the puppy.

The little mouse looked surprised and shook her head.

"Well, think yourself lucky," said the puppy. "Mine did, just because I was a bit rough with my little brother. Would *you* like to be goalkeeper?"

The little mouse took one look at the tangle of puppies on the grass and carried on running. She ran so fast that she almost fell into the duck pond.

"Going for a swim?" quacked a glum voice. The little mouse shook her head.

"Nor me," said the duckling. "I'm not allowed in today, just because I was a bit cheeky. But I could teach *you* how to dive."

The little mouse looked at the other ducklings swimming in the deep, cold pond, and she shivered. Then she carried on running.

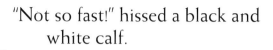

"Not so fast!" hissed a black and white calf.

"I can't stop!" squeaked the little mouse. "I'm running away. Because Mum shouted."

"I wish I could shout!" hissed the calf. "I mooed a bit too loudly last night, and now I'm only allowed to *whisper!*"

"Wow! Was all that noise *you?*" cried the little mouse. "You woke everyone up. We were so frightened that Mum had to bring us a midnight feast and tell us another…"

Suddenly the little mouse felt so homesick that she ran—*whoosh*—all the way back to her hole. She dived straight into bed with her brothers and sisters, and was just in time for a… story!

The Chewalong Song

Chew, chew, I *do* love a chew!
There's nothing like breakfast
All covered in dew.
There's no need to buy it,
Or even to fry it,
So why don't you try it
And *chew*!

Munch, munch, I *do* love a munch!
There's nothing like clover
For flavouring lunch.
Although it grows thickly
You won't find it sickly,
So gather some quickly
And *munch*!

Graze, graze, I *do* love a graze!
There's nothing quite like it
On warm, sunny days.
So please share my dinner,
This field is a winner!
We'll never grow thinner,
Let's *graze*!

A Balloon for Katie Kitten

K atie Kitten loved balloons. When she saw the balloon man in the park, she squealed with delight.

"Please, Mum," she begged, "*please* buy me a balloon."

But Mum wasn't sure. "Those balloons are filled with a gas called helium," she told Katie. "You have to hold on to them very tightly. If you let go, they just float away. Do you think you're grown up enough for a helium balloon?"

"Yes," said Katie, "I *am* grown up enough. *Please* may I have one? I'd like *that* one!" She pointed to a panda balloon.

Mum sighed and got out her purse. The balloon
man beamed and unwound Panda's string. He
wanted to tie the string round Katie's wrist, but Katie
couldn't wait. She ran round and round the park with Panda,
whooping and shouting joyfully.

"Hold tight, Katie Kitten!" warned Mum.

But... *whoosh!* Mum's warning was too late. Panda was already
floating up into a tree.

Katie didn't like heights, but she bravely climbed the tree and
rescued Panda. Mum waited anxiously below.

"I thought you might not be grown up
enough," said Mum, when Katie was
safely on the ground again. "Now, let
me hold Panda. We have shopping to do."

When they got to the department store, Katie grabbed Panda's string and jumped on the escalator. As they rode upstairs, they had a wonderful view of all the things for sale on each floor.

"Wow, look at those toys!" cried Katie. She pointed to a row of dinosaurs, and... *whoosh!* Off went Panda again.

Panda flew past the toys. He flew past the lamps. He flew past the pots and pans, and came to rest right at the top of the store.

At last Mum and Katie got to the top, too.

"I thought you might not be grown up enough..." began Mum.

"There's Panda!" cried Katie. "He's sitting on one of the hats!"

The shop assistant looked very stern. But Katie bravely walked up to her and asked, very politely, if she could get her balloon.

They were just in time. A woman was pointing to the display and asking if she could try on "the cute hat with the panda on top"!

Katie held Panda very tightly while Mum did her shopping. She hung on hard while they waited for the bus. And when they walked up Katie's street, she decided to wrap the string round her wrist.

"Panda can live in my room," she told Mum.

Suddenly baby Jack from next door ran over to greet them. Jack laughed and pointed at Panda. But then he tripped and bumped his nose!

Katie ran to pick him up. "Don't cry, Jack," she said, and gave him a hug.

174

"Oh no!" cried Katie. Panda was floating far, far away. And this time there was nothing to stop him!

As soon as Jack stopped crying, Katie ran inside and shut herself in her room. She wouldn't come downstairs for supper. She didn't want to read or draw or play dominoes.

Brr-ring! went the doorbell. When Katie heard it, she hid her head under her pillow.

After a while, Mum called upstairs, "Katie, there's a visitor here to see you."

But Katie just sniffled and replied, "I'm not… grown up enough… for visitors!"

"Nonsense!" boomed a friendly voice. It was Grandpa Purr. Mum had told him all about their adventures.

"If you're grown up enough to climb a tree without getting hurt," said Grandpa, "and to speak politely to a stern shop assistant, and to comfort baby Jack – then you're grown up enough for me!"

Katie thought about what Grandpa had said. She began to feel a bit better. At last she came downstairs.

"Hold tight, Katie Kitten," said Grandpa. He opened his arms wide to scoop her up and give her a cuddle. But he let go of the balloon he had brought her!

Whooosh! Elephant floated all the way upstairs, right into Katie's room. Grandpa, Mum and Katie all looked at one another and started laughing.

"Oh, Grandpa," cried Katie, "I don't think you're grown up enough for a helium balloon!"

Just the Job for a Dragon

Dilys read the advertisement in the café window:

WANTED
Smart
young lady
to wait
at table

"Just the job for a dragon," thought Dilys, and she stepped inside.

The café manager wasn't so sure. "We'll have to see how you get on," he said.

Dilys helped the cook to peel the potatoes. Then she flew round setting the tables.

At twelve o'clock the first customers arrived. "Oh no," said the manager. "It's the Grumble family! They're never satisfied with *anything!*"

Dilys wasn't worried. She stood by their table with a notepad and pencil, ready to take their orders.

"I can feel a draught," said Grandma Grumble. "It's right on my feet."

"I *am* sorry, Madam," said Dilys. She lifted the cloth and took a deep breath… *PUFF!…* Dilys blew hot air all over Grandma Grumble's toes.

"Ooh, that's lovely!" gurgled Grandma Grumble.

The Grumbles read the menu. "It all sounds horrible," said Mr Grumble. But they ordered a huge meal, just the same.

Dilys brought out their plates. Mr and Mrs Grumble poked and prodded. "These plates are cold!" they cried. "Hot food should be served on hot plates!"

"I do apologise, sir *and* madam," said Dilys. She collected all the plates and turned her back. *Puff!* She aimed a great flame right at the plates, and took them back to the table.

"Ouch!" cried Mr and Mrs Grumble. "That's better! These plates are piping hot now!"

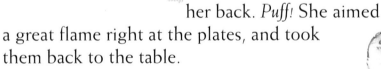

When the Grumbles had finished their main course, Sidney wanted his pudding.

"Bring me a Spaceship Special," he cried. "Banana, jelly, ice cream, syrup, nuts…"

The cook made up the Spaceship Special – but he forgot to light the sparkler on top.

"My sparkler's not lit!" wailed Sidney.

"Oh yes, it is!" said Dilys. *Puff!* She sent a gentle flame right onto the spaceship, and the sparkler crackled into life.

"Crikey!" said Sidney.

The Grumbles paid their bill with hardly a grumble, and Dilys began to clear the table.

"What do you think?" she asked the manager when she had finished.

"I think," said the manager, "that this is *just the job for a dragon!*"

Everard's Ears

Once there was a bunny called Everard who had extra-large ears.

"Everard, your ears are *enormous!*" laughed his friends Basil and Beech.

Everard's ears started drooping, and he looked very unhappy.

"It's all right, son," said Everard's dad. "You just haven't grown into your ears yet. And who knows—one day you may find they come in useful."

But Everard couldn't think of a single thing that big ears would ever be useful for. And it seemed his friends would *never* stop teasing him.

"Shouldn't you put flashing lights on your ears to warn low-flying aircraft?" asked Basil.

"No wonder there's a hole in the ozone layer!" giggled Beech.

Everard's ears drooped down even further.

"Ears up, son," said Everard's dad. "Any rabbit can have ordinary ears, but you're my *extraordinary* Everard. And don't you forget it!"

Now, there was a big cabbage field nearby, and whenever there was washing up or bedroom tidying to be done, Everard, Basil and Beech would hop off into the field to hide. They would sit among the huge cabbages, nibbling leaves or playing games, and wait until they thought it was safe to go home.

One afternoon in the cabbage field, Beech started laughing. "Everard!" he giggled, holding two big cabbage leaves above his head. "What do these remind you of?"

Everard didn't think it was funny. He chased Beech through the cabbages until they were both out of breath.

"Stop!" puffed Basil, trailing along behind. "Where are we?" The cabbages had grown so high that the bunnies couldn't see which way to go.

After what seemed like hours of running in all directions, the three bunnies were near to tears. "We'll be here for *ever*!" said Beech. "I'm sorry, Everard, it's all my fault!"

The frightened little bunnies were exhausted and flopped down among the cabbages. "No one will ever find us," sobbed Basil. "But if we ever do get out, we promise never to make fun of you-know-what again, Everard!"

A few minutes later they heard a cheery voice nearby. "Come on, boys," said Everard's dad. "I'll show you the way home. It's lucky I reached you before it got dark."

"How ever did you find us?" asked Beech, as they all tramped home together.

Everard's dad looked down at his son's ears waving above the cabbages. He gave Everard a big wink. "Let's just say I had *extraordinary* good luck," he said.

Scaredy Kitten

On the night before Christmas, Prescott was all bundled up, ready to go carol singing with his sister Sylvia and their friends. He opened the front door and peered outside.

"Gosh!" he thought. "It's dark. Very dark."

"It's too cold for me," Prescott said to Sylvia.

"It is not," Sylvia said. "You're just afraid of the dark. What a scaredy kitten!"

Prescott went to his room and took off his scarf and hat and mittens and boots. He put on his pyjamas, turned on his night light and crawled into bed.

"Oh no!" he said suddenly. "How could I forget?"

He got out of bed and pulled the window blind down tight. Then he drew the curtains, to make sure he couldn't see the night.

Prescott *was* afraid of the dark. He couldn't tell where the darkness ended and everything else began. He felt as if he were disappearing in the dark. And that made him very nervous.

Most of the time it didn't matter that Prescott was afraid of the dark. But sometimes it mattered a lot.

On Halloween, Prescott got into his ghost costume, ready for trick-or-treating. He thought that maybe the bright white sheet would help keep him from disappearing in the dark.

But when he stepped outside, he saw that it was rainy and foggy, and *very* dark. *Everything* had disappeared!

"It's too wet for me," said Prescott, going back inside.

"Scaredy kitten!" said Sylvia.

Prescott stayed indoors that night and greeted the other trick-or-treaters at the door. They were all smiling or laughing. Prescott hid his sad face behind his mask.

Just a few days later it was Bonfire Night. Everyone was going to the village green to watch the fireworks. Everyone except Prescott.

"I'm too sleepy," said Prescott, pretending to yawn. "Maybe I'll watch from my bedroom window."

"Scaredy kitten!" said Sylvia.

Prescott went up to his room and tried to watch the fireworks from the window. But he ended up turning on his night light, pulling the blind down and drawing the curtains to keep out the night. He never saw any fireworks at all.

A few weeks later it was Prescott's birthday. His grandpa came to his party and brought a special present. When Prescott opened the box, he didn't know what it was.

"This is a telescope," Grandpa explained. "You take it outside at night and look through it to see the sky up close. You'll be surprised when you see what's up there. But we have to wait until it's dark."

Prescott didn't want to be surprised in the dark. He didn't want to go outside at night at all.

"Scaredy kitten," whispered Sylvia. "I bet you don't go!"

But Prescott loved Grandpa very much, and he couldn't disappoint him. So when it got dark, he went outside with Grandpa and the telescope. He held Grandpa's hand very tightly.

Grandpa showed Prescott how to hold the telescope up to his eye and look up at the sky. "Just look through it and tell me what you see," he said to Prescott.

Prescott looked.

"I see stars," he said. "Oh! Look at them! They're so shiny! And look at the moon! The moon is so bright! It's like a huge torch! Wow!"

Prescott was amazed. And when he took the telescope away from his eye, the night didn't seem so dark any more.

"Is the moon there every night?" he asked.

"Yes," replied Grandpa. "On cloudy or foggy nights you can't see the moon or the stars, but they're always there. You can count on them!"

"I can?" Prescott asked.

Grandpa smiled. "Yes," he said. "I knew you'd be surprised. I'll bet you didn't know there was so much light in the night."

When Prescott went to bed that night, he didn't turn on his night light or pull down his window blind or draw the curtains. The stars shone in the window and the moon gleamed brightly.

Prescott smiled as he watched the light of the night glowing in his room. He wasn't afraid of the dark any more.

The Puppy
Who Wanted to Be a Cat

Life seemed far too busy for Penny the puppy. There was always something her parents wanted her to do, and she was fed up with it. So one day, Penny decided to be… a cat.

"Cats can do whatever they like," Penny said to her brother and sister. "I mean, just look at Ginger!"

Penny and her family shared the house with Ginger the cat. He did an awful lot of dozing and was never, ever, in a hurry.

"But you're a dog," said Penny's brother. "You can't be a cat."

"Oh, can't I?" said Penny. "We'll soon see about that!"

From then on, Penny copied everything Ginger did. She walked like a cat, stretched out on the rug like a cat, and even tried to miaow like a cat, although that was quite hard.

And when her parents told her to do something, she said, "I'm sorry, I can't do that. I'm a cat!"

As you can imagine, after a while this started to drive her parents *crazy*. So they came up with a plan…

The next morning there was a surprise for Penny. At breakfast, her brother's bowl was full of lovely, chunky dog food, and so was her sister's. But Penny's contained something rather strange.

"What's *this?*" asked Penny, sniffing at it.

"Well, since you're a cat now," said her mother, "we thought you ought to have cat food for your meals!"

Suddenly Penny wasn't so sure being a cat was such a good idea. How could Ginger eat this disgusting stuff? It was so *yucky...*

The rest of the family burst out laughing at the look on Penny's face. Penny laughed too when her father took away the bowl of cat food and produced a proper breakfast for her.

And from then on Penny was a puppy again. At least she was — until she saw a bird flying through the sky.

"Don't be absurd," said her sister. "You can't be a bird!"

But Penny's parents wouldn't put anything past her.

And neither would I!

Crocodiles *Do* Climb Trees

"Don't do that, Mum," said Snappy. "Crocodiles aren't meant to dance. They're meant to slither and be menacing."

But Snappy's mum didn't want to slither. And she didn't feel at all menacing.

"Slow, slow, quick quick, slow," she hummed as she danced up to a bush filled with flowers. She picked a bright red flower and put it behind her ear.

Snappy groaned. "Leave it out, Mum. What if any of my friends see you?"

Snappy's mum didn't mind *who* saw her. She carried on dancing all afternoon. Then, instead of slithering in a nice, menacing sort of way, she shot up the nearest tree.

"Mum, Mum!" shrieked Snappy. "Crocodiles *don't* climb trees!"

"This one does," said Mum. "It makes me feel good. And I like the view."

Snappy stomped off to the river bank and sulked.

"Come on in!" called a voice from the water. "It's a lovely day for a dip."

Snappy slithered down the bank. He liked the look of this new friend.

"He's just my sort of croc," thought Snappy. And, before he knew it, Snappy had invited him over… the next afternoon.

All night long Snappy worried and wriggled. However could he make his mum behave in front of his new friend? At last he thought of a plan.

At the crack of dawn, Snappy swung into action.

"Wake up, Mum!" he cried. "We'll dance all morning!" That way, Snappy thought, she would be too tired to dance that afternoon!

"Slow, slow, quick quick, slow." Snappy and his mum danced themselves dizzy until lunchtime.

"Let's have lunch in that tree!" cried Snappy. That way, he thought, she wouldn't need to climb it later.

Snappy got Mum back on the ground just in time. "I think I hear someone coming!" he said. "Now please, Mum, remember: crocodiles *don't* climb trees!"

"This one does!" boomed a friendly voice.

Snappy couldn't believe his ears. It was his new friend's mum!

"Slow, slow, quick quick, slow!" She was dancing along in front of her son to show him the way.

Snappy's new friend groaned and blushed. But Snappy gave his widest grin.

"We're going swimming!" he called over his shoulder, as he and his friend slithered off to the river.

But, of course, Snappy's mum didn't hear him. She was too busy showing *her* new friend the view... from her favourite treetop!

NURSERY RHYMES

About the rhymes...

Nursery rhymes are an important part of childhood for every boy and girl. Children of all ages love listening to, reading and joining in with rhymes that take them into a magical world of make-believe. The one hundred and fifty-one rhymes that follow are grouped in four sections, featuring nursery rhyme favourites like *Little Miss Muffet*, playtime rhymes like *Incy Wincy Spider*, number rhymes like *Three Blind Mice* and bedtime rhymes like *Rock-a-bye Baby*.

Contents

Goosey, Goosey, Gander

Goosey, goosey, gander,
    Whither shall I wander?
Upstairs, downstairs,
    In my lady's chamber.
There I met an old man
    Who would not say his prayers.
I took him by the left leg
    And threw him down the stairs.

Jack and Jill

Jack and Jill went up the hill
To fetch a pail of water.
Jack fell down and broke his crown,
And Jill came tumbling after.

Up Jack got, and home did trot,
As fast as he could caper,
To old Dame Dob, who patched his nob
With vinegar and brown paper.

Mary Had a Little Lamb

Mary had a little lamb,
Its fleece was white as snow,
And everywhere that Mary went
The lamb was sure to go.

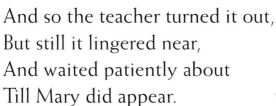

It followed her to school one day,
Which was against the rule.
It made the children laugh and play
To see a lamb at school.

And so the teacher turned it out,
But still it lingered near,
And waited patiently about
Till Mary did appear.

"What makes the lamb love Mary so?"
The eager children cry.
"Why, Mary loves the lamb, you know,"
The teacher did reply.

Baa, Baa, Black Sheep

Baa, baa, black sheep, have you any wool?
Yes, sir, yes, sir, three bags full.
One for the master, and one for the dame,
And one for the little boy who lives in the lane.

Little Boy Blue

Little Boy Blue, come blow your horn!
The sheep's in the meadow, the cow's in the corn.
Where is the boy who looks after the sheep?
He's under the haycock, fast asleep.
Will you wake him? No, not I!
For if I do, he's sure to cry.

Little Bo-peep

Little Bo-peep has lost her sheep,
And doesn't know where to find them.
Leave them alone, and they'll come home,
Bringing their tails behind them.

Little Bo-peep fell fast asleep,
And dreamt she heard them bleating.
But when she awoke, she found it a joke,
For they were still a-fleeting.

Then up she took her little crook,
Determined for to find them.
She found them indeed, but it made her heart bleed,
For they'd left their tails behind them.

Little Bird

Once I saw a little bird
Come hop, hop, hop.
So I cried, "Little bird,
Will you stop, stop, stop?"

I was going to the window
To say, "How do you do?"
But he shook his little tail,
And far away he flew.

Summer Breeze

Summer breeze, so softly blowing,
In my garden pinks are growing.
If you go and send the showers,
You may come and smell my flowers.

Mary, Mary

Mary, Mary, quite contrary,
How does your garden grow?
With silver bells and cockle shells,
And pretty maids all in a row!

Grey Goose and Gander

Grey goose and gander,
      Waft your wings together,
And carry the good King's daughter
      Over the one-strand river.

I Had a Little Nut Tree

I had a little nut tree,
      Nothing would it bear
But a silver nutmeg
      And a golden pear.

The King of Spain's daughter
      Came to visit me,
And all for the sake
      Of my little nut tree.

Bobby Shaftoe

Bobby Shaftoe's gone to sea,
Silver buckles on his knee.
He'll come back and marry me,
Bonny Bobby Shaftoe!

Bobby Shaftoe's fat and fair,
Combing down his yellow hair.
He's my love forevermore,
Bonny Bobby Shaftoe!

Rub-a-Dub-Dub

Rub-a-dub-dub,
Three men in a tub,
And how do you think they got there?
The butcher, the baker,
The candlestick-maker,
They all jumped out of a rotten potato,
'Twas enough to make a man stare.

I Saw a Ship A-Sailing

I saw a ship a-sailing,
     A-sailing on the sea,
And oh, but it was laden
     With pretty things for thee.

There were comfits in the cabin,
     And apples in the hold.
The sails were made of silk,
     And the masts were made of gold.

The four-and-twenty sailors
     That stood between the decks
Were four and twenty white mice
     With chains about their necks.

The captain was a duck
     With a packet on his back,
And when the ship began to move,
     The captain said, "Quack! Quack!"

Old King Cole

Old King Cole was a merry old soul,
And a merry old soul was he.
He called for his pipe, and he called for his bowl,
And he called for his fiddlers three.

Each fiddler he had a fiddle,
And the fiddles went tweedle-dee.
Oh, there's none so rare as can compare
With King Cole and his fiddlers three.

Sing a Song of Sixpence

Sing a song of sixpence,
A pocket full of rye.
Four and twenty blackbirds
Baked in a pie.

When the pie was opened,
The birds began to sing.
Wasn't that a dainty dish
To set before the King?

The King was in the counting house,
Counting out his money.
The Queen was in the parlour,
Eating bread and honey.

The maid was in the garden,
Hanging out the clothes,
When down came a blackbird
And pecked off her nose!

Little Miss Muffet

Little Miss Muffet
Sat on a tuffet,
Eating her curds and whey.
There came a big spider,
Who sat down beside her,
And frightened Miss Muffet away.

Curly Locks

Curly Locks, Curly Locks, wilt thou be mine?
Thou shalt not wash dishes, nor yet feed the swine,
But sit on a cushion and sew a fine seam,
And feast upon strawberries, sugar and cream.

Little Tommy Tucker

Little Tommy Tucker
Sings for his supper.
What shall he eat?
White bread and butter.

How will he cut it
Without e'er a knife?
How will he marry
Without e'er a wife?

Little Jack Horner

Little Jack Horner sat in a corner,
Eating his Christmas pie.
He put in his thumb,
And pulled out a plum,
And said, "What a good boy am I!"

Little Betty Blue

Little Betty Blue
Lost her holiday shoe.
What can little Betty do?
Give her another,
To match the other,
And then she may walk in two.

The Queen of Hearts

The Queen of Hearts,
She made some tarts,
All on a summer's day.
The Knave of Hearts,
He stole the tarts,
And took them clean away.

The King of Hearts
Called for the tarts,
And beat the Knave full sore.
The Knave of Hearts
Brought back the tarts,
And vowed he'd steal no more.

The Lion and the Unicorn

The Lion and the Unicorn
Were fighting for the crown.
The Lion beat the Unicorn
All around the town.
Some gave them white bread,
Some gave them brown,
Some gave them plum cake,
And drummed them out of town.

Humpty Dumpty

Humpty Dumpty sat on a wall,
Humpty Dumpty had a great fall.
    All the King's horses
    And all the King's men
Couldn't put Humpty together again.

Ride a Cockhorse

Ride a cockhorse to Banbury Cross,
To see a fine lady upon a white horse.
Rings on her fingers and bells on her toes,
And she shall have music wherever she goes.

Hickory, Dickory, Dock

Hickory, dickory, dock,
The mouse ran up the clock.
The clock struck one,
The mouse ran down.
Hickory, dickory, dock!

Pussy Cat, Pussy Cat

Pussy cat, pussy cat, where have you been?
"I've been to London to visit the Queen."
Pussy cat, pussy cat, what did you there?
"I frightened a little mouse under the chair."

Six Little Mice

Six little mice sat down to spin,
Pussy passed by, and she peeped in.
What are you doing, my little men?
"We're weaving shirts for gentlemen."
Can I come in and cut off your threads?
"No, no, Mistress Pussy, you'd cut off our heads!"

I Love Little Pussy

I love little pussy, her coat is so warm,
And if I don't hurt her, she'll do me no harm.
So I'll not pull her tail, nor drive her away,
But pussy and I very gently will play.

Jack Sprat

Jack Sprat could eat no fat,
His wife could eat no lean,
And so between them both,
They licked the platter clean.

Jack ate all the lean,
Joan ate all the fat.
The bone they picked clean,
Then gave it to the cat.

Old Mother Hubbard

Old Mother Hubbard
Went to the cupboard
To fetch her poor dog a bone.
But when she got there
The cupboard was bare,
And so the poor dog had none.

There Was an Old Woman

There was an old woman tossed up in a blanket,
    Seventeen times as high as the moon.
But where she was going no mortal could tell,
    For under her arm she carried a broom.
"Old woman, old woman, old woman," said I,
    "Whither, oh whither, oh whither so high?"
"To sweep the cobwebs from the sky,
    And I'll be with you by and by!"

Hey, Diddle, Diddle

Hey, diddle, diddle,
The cat and the fiddle,
The cow jumped over the moon.
The little dog laughed
To see such sport,
And the dish ran away with the spoon!

The Man in the Moon Came Tumbling Down

The man in the moon came tumbling down,
And asked the way to Norwich.
He went by south, and burnt his mouth
With supping cold pease porridge.

Pease Porridge Hot

Pease porridge hot,
Pease porridge cold,
Pease porridge in the pot,
Nine days old.

Some like it hot,
Some like it cold,
Some like it in the pot,
Nine days old.

One Misty, Moisty Morning

One misty, moisty morning,
When cloudy was the weather,
I met with an old man
Clothed all in leather,
Clothed all in leather,
With cap under his chin.
"How do you?" and "How do you do?"
And "How do you do?" again.

Doctor Foster

Doctor Foster went to Gloucester
    In a shower of rain.
He stepped in a puddle, right up to his middle,
    And never went there again.

The Old Woman Who Lived in a Shoe

There was an old woman who lived in a shoe,
She had so many children she didn't know what to do.
She gave them some broth without any bread,
Then scolded them soundly and sent them to bed.

Peter, Peter, Pumpkin Eater

Peter, Peter, pumpkin eater,
Had a wife and couldn't keep her.
He put her in a pumpkin shell,
And there he kept her very well.

Peter, Peter, pumpkin eater,
Had another, and didn't love her.
Peter learned to read and spell,
And then he loved her very well.

Georgie Porgie

Georgie Porgie, pudding and pie,
Kissed the girls and made them cry.
When the boys came out to play,
Georgie Porgie ran away.

Tweedledum and Tweedledee

Tweedledum and Tweedledee
        Agreed to fight a battle,
For Tweedledum said Tweedledee
        Had spoilt his nice new rattle.
Just then flew by a monstrous crow
        As big as a tar barrel,
Which frightened both the heroes so,
        They quite forgot their quarrel.

How Many Days?

How many days has my baby to play?
Saturday, Sunday, Monday,
Tuesday, Wednesday, Thursday, Friday,
Saturday, Sunday, Monday.
Hop away, skip away,
My baby wants to play,
My baby wants to play every day!

Dance to Your Daddy

Dance to your daddy,
My little babby,
Dance to your daddy,
My little lamb!

You shall have a fishy
In a little dishy,
You shall have a fishy
When the boat comes in!

Catch Him, Crow

Catch him, crow! Carry him, kite!
Take him away till the apples are ripe.
When they are ripe and ready to fall,
Here comes baby, apples and all!

Up, Up, Up

Here we go up, up, up.
And here we go down, down, down.
Here we go backwards and forwards,
And here we go round and round!

Dance, Little Baby

Dance, little baby, dance up high!
Never mind, baby, Mother is by.
Crow and caper, caper and crow,
There, little baby, there you go.
Up to the ceiling, down to the ground,
Backwards and forwards, round and round!
Dance little baby, and Mother shall sing,
With the merry chorus, ding-a-ding, ding.

Clap, Clap Handies

Clap, clap handies,
Mummy's wee one.
Clap, clap handies,
Till Daddy comes home,
Home to his bonny wee baby.
Clap, clap handies,
My bonny wee one.

Pat-a-Cake

Pat-a-cake, pat-a-cake, baker's man!
Bake me a cake as fast as you can.
Roll it and pat it and mark it with "B",
And put it in the oven for baby and me.

Five Little Mice

This little mousie peeped within,
This little mousie walked right in!
This little mousie came to play,
This little mousie ran away!
This little mousie cried, "Dear me!
Dinner is done and it's time for tea!"

Two Little Dickey Birds

Two little dickey birds sat upon a hill,
One named Jack, the other named Jill.
Fly away, Jack! Fly away, Jill!
Come again, Jack! Come again, Jill!

Dance, Thumbkin, Dance

Dance, Thumbkin, dance,
Dance, ye merry men, every one.
But Thumbkin, he can dance alone,
Thumbkin, he can dance alone.

Dance, Foreman, dance,
Dance, ye merry men, every one.
But Foreman, he can dance alone,
Foreman, he can dance alone.

Dance, Longman, dance,
Dance, ye merry men, every one,
But Longman, he can dance alone,
Longman, he can dance alone.

Dance, Ringman, dance,
Dance, ye merry men, every one,
But Ringman, he can dance alone,
Ringman, he can dance alone.

Dance, Littleman, dance,
Dance, ye merry men, every one.
But Littleman, he can dance alone,
Littleman, he can dance alone.

Incy Wincy Spider

Incy Wincy Spider climbed up the water spout.
Down came the rain and washed the spider out.
Out came the sunshine, dried up all the rain,
And Incy Wincy Spider climbed up the spout again.

Here Sits the Lord Mayor

Here sits the Lord Mayor,
Here sit two men.
Here sits the cock, and here sits the hen.
Here sit the little chickens,
And here they run in,
Chin-chopper,
Chin-chopper,
Chin-chopper, chin!

Round and Round the Garden

Round and round the garden,
Like a teddy bear.
One step, two steps,
Tickle you under there!

Teddy Bear, Teddy Bear

Teddy bear, teddy bear,
Turn around.
Teddy bear, teddy bear,
Touch the ground.

Teddy bear, teddy bear,
Climb the stairs.
Teddy bear, teddy bear,
Say your prayers.

Teddy bear, teddy bear,
Turn out the light.
Teddy bear, teddy bear,
Say good night.

Jack Be Nimble

Jack be nimble,
Jack be quick.
Jack jump over
The candlestick.

Jumping Joan

Here am I,
Little jumping Joan.
When nobody's with me,
I'm all alone.

Leg Over Leg

Leg over leg,
As the dog went to Dover.
When he came to a stile,
Hop! He went over.

Hogs in the Garden

Hogs in the garden, catch 'em, Towser.
Cows in the cornfield, run, boys, run.
Cats in the cream pot, run, girls, run.
Fire on the mountains, run, boys, run!

See-Saw, Margery Daw

See-saw, Margery Daw,
Jacky shall have a new master.
Jacky shall have but a penny a day,
Because he can't work any faster.

See-Saw, Sacra Down

See-saw, sacra down,
Which is the way to Boston town?
One foot up, the other foot down,
That is the way to Boston town.

This Is the Way the Ladies Ride

This is the way the ladies ride,
Nimble, nimble, nimble, nimble.
This is the way the gentlemen ride,
A gallop, a trot, a gallop, a trot.
This is the way the farmers ride,
Jiggety-jog, jiggety-jog.
And when they come to a hedge – they jump over!
And when they come to a slippery space –
They scramble, scramble, scramble,
Tumble-down Dick!

The Coachman

Up at Piccadilly, oh!
The coachman takes his stand,
And when he meets a pretty girl,
He takes her by the hand.
Whip away for ever, oh!
Drive away so clever, oh!
All the way to Bristol, oh!
He drives her four-in-hand.

Ride, Baby, Ride

Ride, baby, ride,
Pretty baby shall ride,
And have a little puppy dog tied to his side,
And a little pussy cat tied to the other,
And away he shall ride to see his grandmother,
To see his grandmother,
To see his grandmother.

You Ride Behind

You ride behind and I'll ride before,
And trot, trot away to Baltimore.
You shall take bread, and I will take honey,
And both of us carry a purse full of money.

To Market

To market, to market, to buy a fat pig,
Home again, home again, jiggety-jig.
To market, to market, to buy a fat hog,
Home again, home again, jiggety-jog.

This Little Pig

This little pig went to market,
This little pig stayed at home.
This little pig had roast beef,
This little pig had none.
And this little pig cried, "Wee-wee-wee,"
All the way home.

The Blacksmith

"Robert Barnes, my fellow fine,
Can you shoe this horse of mine?"
"Yes, indeed, that I can,
As well as any other man.
There's a nail, and there's a prod,
And now, you see, your horse is shod!"

Cobbler, Cobbler

Cobbler, cobbler, mend my shoe,
Get it done by half-past two.
Do it neat, and do it strong,
And I will pay you when it's done.

I'm a Little Teapot

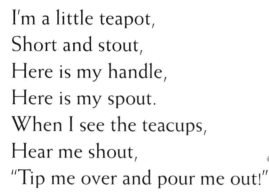

I'm a little teapot,
Short and stout,
Here is my handle,
Here is my spout.
When I see the teacups,
Hear me shout,
"Tip me over and pour me out!"

Polly Put the Kettle On

Polly put the kettle on,
Polly put the kettle on,
Polly put the kettle on,
    We'll all have tea.

Sukey take it off again,
Sukey take it off again,
Sukey take it off again,
    They've all gone away.

Blow the fire and make the toast,
Put the muffins down to roast,
Blow the fire and make the toast,
    We'll all have tea.

Wash the Dishes

Wash the dishes, wipe the dishes,
Ring the bell for tea.
Three good wishes, three good kisses,
I will give to thee.

Handy Pandy

Handy Pandy, Jack-a-dandy,
Loves plum cake and sugar candy.
He bought some at the grocer's shop,
And out he came, hop, hop, hop!

Girls and Boys, Come Out to Play

Girls and boys, come out to play,
The moon is shining bright as day.
Leave your supper and leave your sleep,
And come with your playfellows into the street.
Come with a whoop, and come with a call,
Come with a good will, or come not at all.
Come, let us dance on the open green,
And she who holds longest shall be our queen.

Round About the Rosebush

Round about the rosebush,
    Three steps,
    Four steps,
All the little boys and girls
    Are sitting
    On the doorsteps.

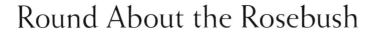

Ring-a-Ring o' Roses

Ring-a-ring o' roses,
A pocket full of posies.
A-tishoo! A-tishoo!
We all fall down!

Here We Go Round the Mulberry Bush

Here we go round the mulberry bush,
    The mulberry bush, the mulberry bush.
Here we go round the mulberry bush,
    On a cold and frosty morning.

This is the way we wash our clothes,
    Wash our clothes, wash our clothes.
This is the way we wash our clothes,
    On a cold and frosty morning.

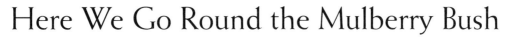

Pop Goes the Weasel!

Up and down the City Road,
    In and out the Eagle,
That's the way the money goes,
    Pop goes the weasel!

Half a pound of tuppenny rice,
    Half a pound of treacle,
Mix it up and make it nice,
    Pop goes the weasel!

Bangalorey Man

Follow my Bangalorey Man,
Follow my Bangalorey Man,
I'll do all that ever I can
To follow my Bangalorey Man.

We'll borrow a horse and steal a gig,
And round the world we'll do a jig,
And I'll do all that ever I can
To follow my Bangalorey Man.

The Muffin Man

Oh, do you know the muffin man,
    The muffin man, the muffin man.
Oh, do you know the muffin man
    That lives in Drury Lane?

Oh, yes, I know the muffin man,
    The muffin man, the muffin man.
Oh, yes, I know the muffin man
    That lives in Drury Lane.

Oranges and Lemons

Oranges and lemons,
Say the bells of St Clement's.

You owe me five farthings,
Say the bells of St Martin's.

When will you pay me?
Say the bells of Old Bailey.

When I grow rich,
Say the bells at Shoreditch.

Pray, when will that be?
Say the bells of Stepney.

I'm sure I don't know,
Says the great bell at Bow.

Here comes a candle to light you to bed,
And here comes a chopper to chop off your head.

London Bridge

London Bridge is falling down,
    Falling down, falling down.
London Bridge is falling down,
    My fair lady.

Build it up with iron bars,
    Iron bars, iron bars.
Build it up with iron bars,
    My fair lady.

Iron bars will bend and break,
    Bend and break, bend and break.
Iron bars will bend and break,
    My fair lady.

Build it up with gold and silver,
    Gold and silver, gold and silver.
Build it up with gold and silver,
    My fair lady.

Gold and silver I've not got,
    I've not got, I've not got.
Gold and silver I've not got,
    My fair lady.

Then off to prison you must go,
    You must go, you must go.
Then off to prison you must go,
    My fair lady.

The Grand Old Duke of York

Oh, the grand old Duke of York,
He had ten thousand men.
He marched them up to the top of the hill,
And he marched them down again.
And when they were up, they were up.
And when they were down, they were down,
And when they were only halfway up,
They were neither up nor down!

The Big Ship Sails

The big ship sails on the alley, alley O,
The alley, alley O, the alley, alley O.
The big ship sails on the alley, alley O,
On the last day of September.

The captain said, "It will never, never do,
Never, never do, never, never do."
The captain said, "It will never, never do,"
On the last day of September.

The big ship sank to the bottom of the sea,
The bottom of the sea, the bottom of the sea.
The big ship sank to the bottom of the sea,
On the last day of September.

We all dip our heads in the deep blue sea,
The deep blue sea, the deep blue sea.
We all dip our heads in the deep blue sea,
On the last day of September.

One, Two, Buckle My Shoe

One, two, buckle my shoe,

Three, four, knock at the door.

Five, six, pick up sticks,

Seven, eight, lay them straight.

Nine, ten, a big fat hen,

Eleven, twelve, dig and delve.

Thirteen, fourteen, maids a-courting,

Fifteen, sixteen, maids in the kitchen.

Seventeen, eighteen, maids in waiting,

Nineteen, twenty, my plate's empty.

One for the Money

One for the money,
Two for the show,
Three to make ready,
And four to go!

I Love Sixpence

I love sixpence, jolly, jolly sixpence,
    I love sixpence as my life.
I spent a penny of it, I spent a penny of it,
    I took a penny home to my wife.

I love fourpence, jolly, jolly fourpence,
    I love fourpence as my life.
I spent twopence of it, I spent twopence of it,
    I took twopence home to my wife.

I love nothing, jolly, jolly nothing,
    I love nothing as my life.
I spent nothing of it, I spent nothing of it,
    I took nothing home to my wife.

My Father, He Left Me

My father, he left me, just as he was able,
One bowl, one bottle, one table,
Two bowls, two bottles, two tables,
Three bowls, three bottles, three tables,
Four bowls, four bottles, four tables,
Five bowls, five bottles, five tables,
Six bowls, six bottles, six tables.

Hot Cross Buns

Hot cross buns!
Hot cross buns!
One a penny, two a penny,
Hot cross buns!
If your daughters do not like them,
Give them to your sons.
One a penny, two a penny,
Hot cross buns!

Hickety, Pickety

Hickety, pickety, my black hen,
She lays eggs for gentlemen.
Sometimes nine, and sometimes ten,
Hickety, pickety, my black hen.

Chook, Chook, Chook

Chook, chook, chook, chook, chook,
Good morning, Mrs Hen.
How many chickens have you got?
Madam, I've got ten.
Four of them are yellow,
And four of them are brown,
And two of them are speckled red,
The nicest in the town.

Magpies

I saw eight magpies in a tree,
Two for you and six for me.
One for sorrow, two for mirth,
Three for a wedding, four for a birth.
Five for England, six for France,
Seven for a fiddler, eight for a dance.

Jenny Wren

Jenny Wren last week was wed,
And built her nest in Grandpa's shed.
Look in next week and you shall see
Two little eggs, and maybe three.

The Dove Says, Coo, Coo

The dove says, "Coo, coo, what shall I do?
I can scarce maintain two."
"Pooh, pooh," says the wren, "I have got ten,
And keep them all like gentlemen."

Three Blind Mice

Three blind mice,
Three blind mice,
See how they run!
See how they run!
They all ran after the farmer's wife,
Who cut off their tails with a carving knife.
Did you ever see such a sight in your life,
As three blind mice?

White Feet

One white foot, buy him,
Two white feet, try him.
Three white feet, wait and see.
Four white feet, let him be.

Barber, Barber

Barber, barber, shave a pig,
How many hairs to make a wig?
Four and twenty, that's enough.
Give the barber a pinch of snuff.

Gregory Griggs

Gregory Griggs, Gregory Griggs,
Had twenty-seven different wigs.
He wore them up, he wore them down,
To please the people of the town.
He wore them east, he wore them west,
But he never could tell which he loved best.

255

Three Young Rats

Three young rats with black felt hats,
Three young ducks with new straw flats,
Three young dogs with curling tails,
Three young cats with demi veils,
Went out to walk with two young pigs
In satin vests and sorrel wigs.
But suddenly it chanced to rain,
And so they all went home again.

As I Was Going to St Ives

As I was going to St Ives,
I met a man with seven wives.
Each wife had seven sacks,
Each sack had seven cats,
Each cat had seven kits.
Kits, cats, sacks, wives,
How many were going to St Ives?

(Answer: Only one — "I".)

Five Little Pussy Cats

Five little pussy cats sitting in a row,
Blue ribbons round each neck, fastened in a bow.
Hey, pussies! Ho, pussies! Are your faces clean?
Don't you know you're sitting there so as to be seen?

One, Two, Three, Four, Five

One, two, three, four, five,
Once I caught a fish alive.
Why did you let it go?
Because it bit my finger so.

Six, seven, eight, nine, ten,
Shall we go to fish again?
Not today, some other time,
For I have broke my fishing line.

Three Wise Men

Three wise men of Gotham
Went to sea in a bowl.
If the bowl had been stronger,
My song would be longer!

I Saw Three Ships

I saw three ships come sailing by,
    Come sailing by, come sailing by.
I saw three ships come sailing by,
    On New Year's Day in the morning!

And what do you think was in them then,
    Was in them then, was in them then?
And what do you think was in them then,
    On New Year's Day in the morning?

Three pretty girls were in them then,
    Were in them then, were in them then.
Three pretty girls were in them then,
    On New Year's Day in the morning.

One could whistle and one could sing,
    And one could play the violin.
Such joy there was at my wedding,
    On New Year's Day in the morning!

One Old Oxford Ox

One old Oxford ox opening oysters,

Two toads, totally tired, trying to trot to Tisbury.

Three thick thumping tigers taking toast for tea,

Four finicky fishermen fishing for finny fish.

Five frippery Frenchmen foolishly fishing for frogs,

Six sportsmen shooting snipe.

Seven Severn salmon swallowing shrimps,

Eight eminent Englishmen eagerly examining Europe.

Nine nimble noblemen nibbling nectarines,

Ten tinkering tinkers tinkering ten tin tinderboxes.

Eleven elephants, elegantly equipped,

Twelve typographical topographers typically translating types.

Mary at the Kitchen Door

One, two, three, four,
Mary at the kitchen door.
Five, six, seven, eight,
Eating cherries off a plate.

One's None

One's none,
Two's some,
Three's many,
Four's a penny,
Five's a little hundred.

Three Little Ghostesses

Three little ghostesses,
Sitting on postesses,
Eating buttered toastesses,
Greasing up their fistesses,
Up to their wristesses.
Oh, what beastesses,
To make such feastesses!

One, Two, Three

One, two, three,
I love coffee,
And Billy loves tea.
How good you be,
One, two, three,
I love coffee,
And Billy loves tea.

There Were Three Cooks

There were three cooks of Colebrook,
And they fell out with our cook.
And all was for the pudding he took
From the three cooks of Colebrook.

Four-Leaf Clover

One leaf for fame, one leaf for wealth,
One for a faithful lover,
And one leaf to bring glorious health,
Are all in a four-leaf clover.

One, He Loves

One, he loves; two, he loves;
Three, he loves, they say.
Four, he loves with all his heart;
Five, he casts away.
Six, he loves; seven, she loves;
Eight, they both love.
Nine, he comes; ten, he tarries;
Eleven, he courts; twelve, he marries.

There Were Two Wrens

There were two wrens upon a tree,
Whistle and I'll come to thee.
Another came, and there were three,
Whistle and I'll come to thee.
Another came, and there were four.
You needn't whistle any more,
For, being frightened, off they flew,
And there are none to show to you.

Two Crows

There were two crows sat on a stone,
One flew away and there was one.
The other, seeing his neighbour gone,
He flew away and then there were none.

Two Cats of Kilkenny

There once were two cats of Kilkenny,
Each thought there was one cat too many.
So they fought and they fit,
And they scratched and they bit,
Till, excepting their nails,
And the tips of their tails,
Instead of two cats, there weren't any.

Twelve Huntsmen

Twelve huntsmen with horns and hounds,
Hunting over other men's grounds.

Eleven ships sailing o'er the main,
Some bound for France and some for Spain,
I wish them all safe home again.

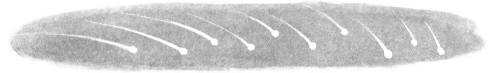

Ten comets in the sky,
Some low and some high.

Nine peacocks in the air,
I wonder how they all came there?
I do not know, and I do not care.

Eight joiners in Joiners' Hall,
Working with their tools and all.

Seven lobsters in a dish,
As fresh as any heart could wish.

Six beetles against the wall,
Close by an old woman's apple stall.

Five puppies of our dog Ball,
Who daily for their breakfast call.

Four horses stuck in a bog,
Three monkeys tied to a clog.

Two pudding-ends would choke a dog,

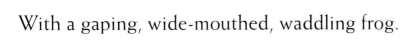

With a gaping, wide-mouthed, waddling frog.

Twinkle, Twinkle

Twinkle, twinkle, little star,
How I wonder what you are!
Up above the world so high,
Like a diamond in the sky.

When the blazing sun is gone,
When he nothing shines upon,
Then you show your little light,
Twinkle, twinkle, all the night.

In the dark blue sky you keep,
And often through my curtains peep,
For you never shut your eye,
Till the sun is in the sky.

Jane Taylor

Star Light

Star light, star bright,
First star I see tonight,
I wish I may, I wish I might,
Have the wish I wish tonight.

I See the Moon

I see the moon,
And the moon sees me.
God bless the moon,
And God bless me.

The Man in the Moon

The Man in the Moon looked out of the moon,
      And this is what he said:
"Now that I'm getting up, 'tis time
      All children went to bed!"

Wee Willie Winkie

Wee Willie Winkie runs through the town,
Upstairs and downstairs in his nightgown,
Rapping at the window, crying through the lock,
"Are the children all in bed, for now it's eight o'clock!"

The Sandman

The Sandman comes,
The Sandman comes.
He has such pretty snow-white sand,
And well he's known throughout the land.
The Sandman comes.

All the Pretty Little Horses

Hush-a-bye, don't you cry,
Go to sleep little baby.
When you wake, you shall have
All the pretty little horses.
Blacks and bays, dapples and greys,
Coach and six little horses.

Bossy-Cow, Bossy-Cow

Bossy-cow, bossy-cow, where do you lie?
In the green meadows, under the sky.

Billy-horse, billy-horse, where do you lie?
Out in the stable, with nobody nigh.

Birdies bright, birdies sweet, where do you lie?
Up in the treetops, ever so high.

Baby dear, baby love, where do you lie?
In my warm cradle, with Mama close by.

Come, Let's to Bed

"Come, let's to bed,"
Says Sleepy-head.
"Tarry awhile," says Slow.
"Put on the pan,"
Says Greedy Nan,
"Let's sup before we go."

A Glass of Milk

A glass of milk and a slice of bread,
And then good night, we must go to bed.

Sippity Sup

Sippity sup, sippity sup,
Bread and milk from a china cup.
Bread and milk from a bright silver spoon,
Made of a piece of the bright silver moon!
Sippity sup, sippity sup,
Sippity, sippity sup!

Go to Bed First

Go to bed first, a golden purse;
Go to bed second, a golden pheasant;
Go to bed third, a golden bird.

Go to Bed Late

Go to bed late,
Stay very small.
Go to bed early,
Grow very tall.

Come to the Window

Come to the window,
My baby, with me,
And look at the stars
That shine on the sea!
There are two little stars
That play at bo-peep
With two little fishes
Far down in the deep,
And two little frogs
Cry, "Neap, neap, neap,
I see a dear baby
That should be asleep!"

Sweet and Low

Sweet and low, sweet and low,
    Wind of the western sea.
Low, low, breathe and blow,
    Wind of the western sea!
Over the rolling waters go,
Come from the dying moon, and blow,
    Blow him again to me;
While my little one, while my pretty one, sleeps.

Sleep and rest, sleep and rest,
    Father will come to thee soon;
Rest, rest, on mother's breast,
    Father will come to thee soon.
Father will come to his babe in the nest,
Silver sails all out of the west,
    Under the silver moon;
Sleep, my little one, sleep, my pretty one, sleep.

Alfred, Lord Tennyson

Up the Wooden Hill

Up the wooden hill
    To Bedfordshire,
Down Sheet Lane
    To Blanket Fair.

Diddle, Diddle, Dumpling

Diddle, diddle, dumpling, my son John
Went to bed with his trousers on.
One shoe off, and one shoe on,
Diddle, diddle, dumpling, my son John.

Babyland

How many miles to Babyland?
Anyone can tell.
Up one flight, to your right,
Please to ring the bell.

What do they do in Babyland?
Dream and wake and play,
Laugh and crow, fonder grow,
Jolly times have they.

Rock-a-bye Baby

Rock-a-bye baby, thy cradle is green,
Father's a nobleman, Mother's a queen.
Betty's a lady and wears a gold ring,
And Johnny's a drummer, and drums for the King.

Hush, Little Baby

Hush, little baby, don't say a word,

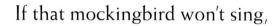

Papa's going to buy you a mockingbird.

If that mockingbird won't sing,

Papa's going to buy you a diamond ring.

If that diamond ring turns brass,

Papa's going to buy you a looking glass.

If that looking glass gets broke,

Papa's going to buy you a billy goat.

If that billy goat won't pull,

Papa's going to buy you a cart and bull.

If that cart and bull turn over,

Papa's going to buy you a dog named Rover.

If that dog named Rover won't bark,

Papa's going to buy you a horse and cart.

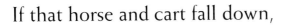

If that horse and cart fall down,

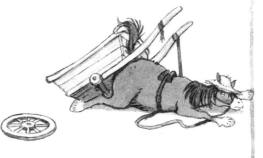

You'll still be the sweetest little baby in town.

French Cradle Song

If my boy sleep quietly,
He shall see the busy bee,
When it has made its honey fine,
Dancing in the bright sunshine.

If my boy will slumber,
Angels without number
Will draw near, so fair and bright,
For they only come at night.

Sleep, Oh Sleep

Sleep, oh sleep,
While breezes so softly are blowing.
Sleep, oh sleep,
While streamlets so gently are flowing.
Sleep, oh sleep!

Sleep, oh sleep,
While birds in the forest are singing.
Sleep, oh sleep,
While echoes with music are ringing.
Sleep, oh sleep!

Sleep, oh sleep,
While angels are watching beside thee.
Sleep, oh sleep,
May blessings for ever betide thee.
Sleep, oh sleep.

Hush-a-bye, Baby

Hush-a-bye, baby, lie still in the cradle,
Mother has gone to buy a soup ladle.
When she comes back, she'll bring us some meat,
And Father and baby shall have some to eat.

Dear Baby, Lie Still

Hush-a-bye, baby, lie still with thy daddy,
Thy mammy has gone to the mill,
To get some meal, to make a cake,
So pray, my dear baby, lie still.

Rock-a-bye, Baby, Rock

Rock-a-bye, baby, rock, rock, rock,
Baby shall have a new pink frock!
A new pink frock and a ribbon to tie,
If baby is good and does not cry.

Rock-a-bye, baby, rock, rock, rock,
Listen, who comes with a knock, knock, knock?
Oh, it is pussy! Come in, come in!
Mother and baby are always at home.

Raisins and Almonds

To my baby's cradle in the night
Comes a little goat all snowy-white.
The goat will trot to the market,
While Mother her watch does keep,
Bringing back raisins and almonds.
Sleep, my little one, sleep.

Hush-a-bye, Baby, on the Treetop

Hush-a-bye, baby, on the treetop,
When the wind blows, the cradle will rock.
When the bough breaks, the cradle will fall,
And down will come baby, cradle and all.

Sleep, Baby, Sleep

Sleep, baby, sleep,
Thy father guards the sheep,
Thy mother shakes the dreamland tree,
And from it fall sweet dreams for thee.
Sleep, baby, sleep.

Sleep, baby, sleep,
Our cottage vale is deep.
The little lamb is on the green,
With woolly fleece so soft and clean.
Sleep, baby, sleep.

Sleep, baby, sleep,
Down where the woodbines creep.
Be always like the lamb so mild,
A kind and sweet and gentle child.
Sleep, baby, sleep.

Cradle Song

Lullaby and good night, with roses bedight,
With lilies bedecked is baby's wee bed.
Lay thee down now and rest,
May thy slumber be blessed.
Lay thee down now and rest,
May thy slumber be blessed.

Lullaby and good night, thy mother's delight,
Bright angels around my darling shall stand.
They will guard thee from harms,
Thou shalt wake in my arms.
They will guard thee from harms,
Thou shalt wake in my arms.

Johannes Brahms

The Evening Is Coming

The evening is coming, the sun sinks to rest,
The birds are all flying straight home to the nest.
"Caw," says the crow as he flies overhead,
"It's time little children were going to bed!"

The butterfly, drowsy, has folded its wing.
The bees are returning, no more the birds sing.
Their labour is over, their nestlings are fed.
It's time little children were going to bed.

Here comes the pony, his work is all done,
Down through the meadow he takes a good run.
Up go his heels and down goes his head.
It's time little children were going to bed.

Now the Day Is Over

Now the day is over,
Night is drawing nigh.
Shadows of the evening
Steal across the sky.

Down with the Lambs

Down with the lambs,
    Up with the lark,
Run to bed, children,
    Before it gets dark.

Quiet the Night

Quiet the night,
Soft is the breeze.
Dim is the light
Of the faraway moon.

Sleep, children, sleep,
Be not alarmed,
Angels on guard
Will keep you unharmed.

Golden Slumbers

Golden slumbers kiss your eyes,
Smiles awake you when you rise.
Sleep, pretty baby, do not cry,
And I will sing you a lullaby.
Rock them, rock them, lullaby.

Good Night

Good night,
Sleep tight,
Wake up bright
In the morning light
To do what's right
With all your might.

NURSERY
TALES

About the stories...

Children of all ages love traditional nursery tales. They always have, and they always will! What makes these stories extra special is that whatever the make-believe adventures, dangers and problems, there is always a happy ending! The twenty nursery tales that follow represent the best of traditional stories retold in a lively style, and include favourites like *The Three Little Pigs*, *Snow White and the Seven Dwarfs*, *Little Red Riding Hood* and *The Ugly Duckling*.

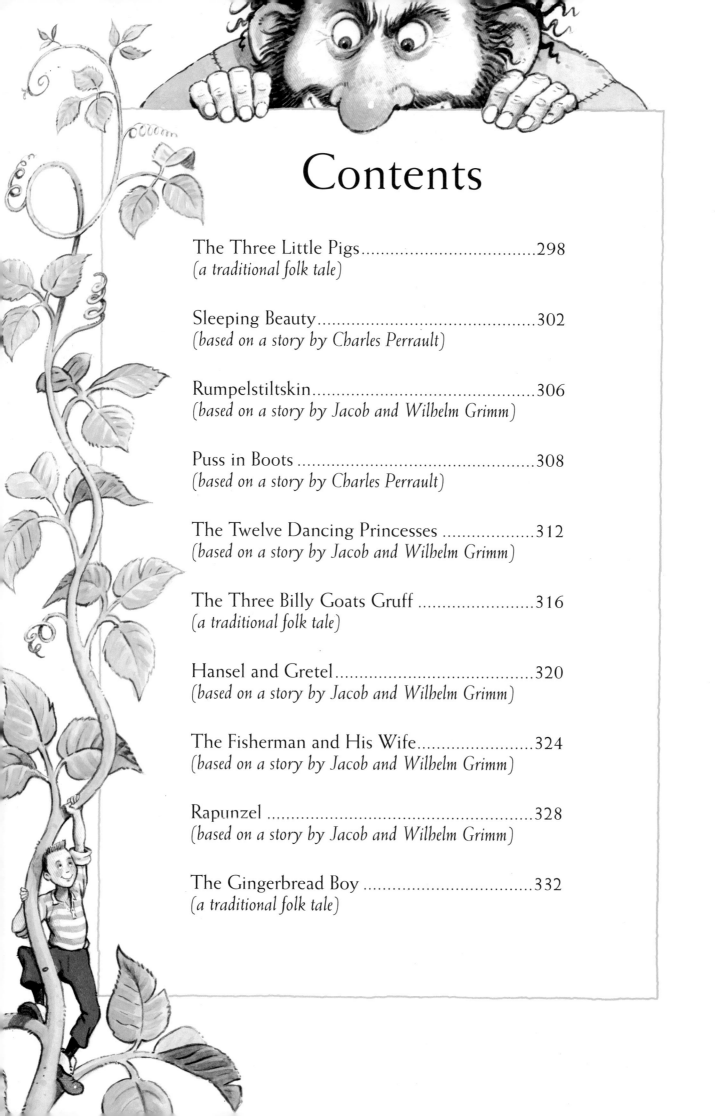

Contents

The Three Little Pigs

Once three little pigs decided it was about time they left home and found their own place to live. No sooner said than done. That very morning they packed up their things, kissed their mother goodbye, and set off.

They walked till midday. Then they sat by the road and ate half their sandwiches. After a nap they set off again. By suppertime the first little pig felt too tired to go any further.

"But we haven't got anywhere yet!" his brother and sister said. "What are you going to do for a house?"

They were next to a field full of wheat that had just been cut. "I'll build a house out of straw," the little pig said. He closed his eyes and went straight to sleep.

When the first little pig woke, the sun was sinking fast and the air was growing cold. And what was that dark hairy shadow in the wood? Suddenly he wished he'd gone on with the others. But he set to work, gathered together some straw, and built his house.

At midnight there came a tapping at his door. "Little pig, little pig, let me come in," a voice said. The little pig's blood ran cold. Now he knew what the shadow had been — a wolf!

"You're not coming in here, not by the hair on my chinny-chin-chin," he said in his most grown-up voice.

"Then I'll huff and I'll puff and I'll blow your house in!" the wolf snarled. "And that'll be the end of you." And it was.

Next morning the other pigs came back. What did they find? A heap of straw and all their brother's belongings torn up and scattered across the field. They ran away as quickly as they could.

By midday the two little pigs were exhausted and stopped running. The second little pig began to think that they had reached a very nice spot. There was a pile of wood that a woodcutter had left, perfect for building a big strong house.

"Whatever happened to my brother can never happen to me," thought the second little pig. But that night, as the church clock struck twelve, there came a tapping at her door.

"Little pig, little pig, let me come in," a voice said softly. "I'm lonely and hungry. I want a bite to eat."

The little pig's heart gave a thump. Now she knew what had happened to her brother. "Wolf! You don't fool me! You're not coming in, not by the hair on my chinny-chin-chin!" she cried.

"Then I'll huff and I'll puff and I'll blow your house in!" the wolf snarled. "And that'll be the end of you." And it was.

Next morning the third little pig found the wooden house shattered to pieces and all his sister's possessions blowing in the wind. He began to run away but then he thought, "What did my sister and I pass down the road yesterday? A brick factory!" Back he went and bought enough bricks to build a house.

That night the wolf came prowling and tapping again. "I'm a friend of your brother and sister," he called. "Little pig, little pig, let me come in."

"Wolf, you're not coming in here, not by the hair on my chinny-chin-chin!" the third little pig shouted.

"Then I'll huff and I'll puff and I'll blow your house in!" the wolf snarled. He drew a deep breath and huffed and puffed with all his might. A wind that would have torn up whole woods hit the house, but the walls stood firm because they were built of bricks. The wolf huffed and puffed again and again, but only the doors and windows rattled. In a towering rage, the wolf leapt up onto the roof and began to climb down the chimney.

But the third little pig had thought of this. He quickly built a roaring fire in the grate and put a huge pot of water on to boil. Instead of landing in the fireplace, the wolf fell into the pot and was boiled up. His skin popped open and out jumped the little pig's brother and sister! The wolf had gobbled them whole!

How happy the three little pigs were to see each other again! Safe and sound, in the house built of bricks, they lived happily ever after.

Sleeping Beauty

Once a king and queen gave an enormous party to celebrate the birth of their daughter. After the feast the King told everyone how happy he was to be a father, for he and his wife had been waiting for years to have a child. Next he made everyone laugh with his story about learning to change nappies. Then it was time for the guests to give the baby princess their presents.

The last to come forward with their gifts were twelve fairies. "My gift to the princess is Happiness," the first fairy announced. The guests clapped and the King beamed all over his face.

"Mine is Beauty," said the second. "Mine Wisdom," said the third. And so they went on.

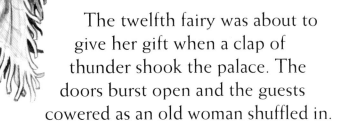

The twelfth fairy was about to give her gift when a clap of thunder shook the palace. The doors burst open and the guests cowered as an old woman shuffled in.

"The thirteenth fairy!" people gasped in horror.

The fairy's terrible voice hissed from the doorway, "Where's my invitation, King?"

"Someone must have forgotten to deliver it," the King mumbled. "Servants! Set another place! Quick!" Actually he hadn't invited her because he only had twelve golden plates for the fairies to eat from, so he'd decided to leave one out.

The fairy stood over the little princess's cradle. The baby gurgled and reached up her tiny hand. Suddenly the fairy cackled, "My gift is that on the princess's fifteenth birthday she will prick her finger on a spindle and die!"

With another clap of thunder the wicked fairy flew away. The palace doors banged shut. There was a terrible silence. Then the Queen began to cry.

The twelfth fairy stepped forward. "I have not given my present yet," she said softly. "I can't undo the evil spell, but I can change it. My gift will be that instead of dying, the princess will sleep for a hundred years."

Years passed and all went well. The baby grew into a healthy young girl, pretty and happy and clever. The King and Queen no longer thought about the evil spell. All the spindles in the land had long been destroyed. Surely the princess was safe.

But on the very day of her fifteenth birthday, the princess found a door she'd never noticed before. Behind it a staircase climbed into a tower. Up the princess went until she reached a door with a golden key. The princess entered a tiny room. An old lady sat at a wheel. "What are you doing?" the princess asked. The old lady smiled. "I'm spinning! Don't stand there staring, child. Try it yourself." She pushed the spindle towards the princess.

At that moment a terrible thing happened. The sharp spindle pricked the princess's finger and she sank to the floor. Down in the busy courtyard the hens stopped cackling. The princess's dog stopped chasing the cook's cat. In his study the King was writing his daughter's birthday card but the pen fell from his fingers. Even the kitchen fire stopped burning. The whole palace went to sleep.

Years slowly passed. The palace was forgotten. But a hundred years later a handsome young prince happened to ride by. He noticed a thorny hedge growing high in the distance. His servants laughed and told him an old story of an enchanted palace and a sleeping beauty. "But what if it's true?" the prince thought and rode towards the hedge.

At first he could see no way through. The hedge was far too thick and thorny for climbing. Then he drew his sword and began to hack his way in. The prince couldn't believe what he found on the far side. All round him animals and people stood and lay as still as statues. He walked through the palace. Not even a fly buzzed on the sunlit windows. No one moved. No one answered his questions.

Then he came to a half-open door at the base of a tower. Inside was a staircase. The prince thought he saw something gold glinting at the top. He bounded up the steps and a moment later was beside the princess. "Sleeping Beauty," he murmured to himself, leaning over her. He couldn't resist. He bent down and kissed her on the lips.

At once the princess opened her eyes. As she did so, the fire roared back into life down in the kitchen. In his study the King picked up the pen he'd dropped and finished writing his daughter's birthday card. The hens pecked for grain in the dust.

And in the room at the top of the tower, the princess saw the prince's face above her. For the first time in a hundred years she smiled. "Will you marry me?" the prince whispered. "Yes!" the princess said, and she kissed him back. When the King heard the good news, he ordered an *enormous* feast. The prince and princess were married and they lived happily ever after.

Rumpelstiltskin

Once a poor miller had a clever, beautiful daughter. One day he boasted to the King that his daughter could spin straw into gold. Of course this wasn't true, but the King believed him. So he locked the miller's daughter in a room full of straw and said that if she did not spin it all into gold by next morning, he would chop off her head.

The girl was sitting there weeping, not even trying to spin, when a voice said, "What will you give me if I do your job?" A strange little man was in the room.

"My necklace," said the girl. And the little man spun the straw into gold.

Next day the King locked the girl into an even bigger room. Again the little man appeared. This time the girl gave him a ring in return for his work.

The third day, the King promised to marry the girl if she did the trick one last time. He locked her into a room as big as a barn. When the little man appeared, the girl had nothing to give.

"In that case," he said, "when you are Queen your firstborn will be mine." Secretly the girl thought *Never!* All the same, she let the little man do his magic spinning.

The King was as good as his word and
they were married. In a year's time, the new
Queen had her first baby. How horrified she
was when the little man appeared. She offered him gold but no,
he would only have the baby. The Queen wept so hard that he
took pity on her. He said that if she could guess his name in three
nights, she could keep her baby.

The first night she went all through the alphabet: Aaron,
Bartholomew, Christian… None of her guesses was right.

The second night she tried funny-sounding names: Artitickle,
Danielslovel, Gumdroopy… But again she was wrong each time.

Then the Queen overheard a servant laughing about a strange
little man he'd seen in the forest dancing and chanting to himself,

"My name's not Elgin, Merlin, Finn or Larkin!
My secret name is Rumpelstiltskin!"

When the little man realized that the Queen
knew what he was called, he flew into such a rage
that smoke came out of his ears and he stamped his
foot through the floorboards. In his effort to pull
himself out, he split into two. And that was
the end of him!

Puss in Boots

Once there was a miller who had three sons. When he died, he left his mill to the eldest son and his donkey to the second son. The youngest got Puss. This made him most unhappy.

"What can you do with a cat?" he protested. "Cats don't even make a decent stew." Puss overheard that and spoke up quickly. "You'll find you haven't got such a bad bargain, Master. Just give me a bag and a pair of boots and you'll see what I can do for you."

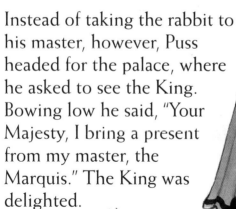

Surprised, the boy did as the cat asked. Puss pulled on the boots and admired himself in the mirror. Then he took a lettuce and a juicy carrot from the pantry and marched off into the woods. There he opened the bag, arranged the lettuce and carrot inside, and hid nearby. Soon a tender young rabbit came along. He smelt the tasty vegetables and hopped inside the bag. In a second, Puss leapt up and tied the bag up tight.

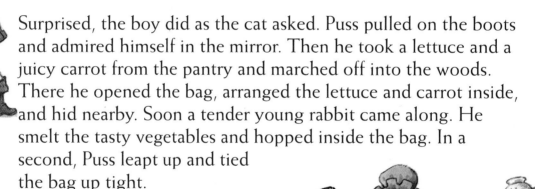

Instead of taking the rabbit to his master, however, Puss headed for the palace, where he asked to see the King. Bowing low he said, "Your Majesty, I bring a present from my master, the Marquis." The King was delighted.

For three months Puss brought so many presents to the palace that the King began to look forward to seeing him. Then at last the day Puss had been waiting for arrived. "Don't ask any questions, Master," he said, "but go and bathe in the river this morning." Puss knew that the King would be driving nearby with the Princess, his daughter.

Later that morning, as the King's carriage drew near the river, Puss came rushing up all a-tremble. "Help! Help!" he gasped. "The Marquis, my master, is drowning!" Immediately the King sent a regiment of soldiers to the rescue.

But Puss had not finished. He told the King that while his master had been swimming, robbers had stolen his clothes. (In fact, Puss had hidden his master's rags in some bushes himself!) The King lost no time in sending for a suit of clothes for the Marquis. As you can imagine, Puss's master was feeling very bewildered at his sudden change of name, but he was clever enough to keep quiet.

As soon as the Marquis was decently dressed, the King invited him to ride in his carriage and meet his daughter. The Princess took one look at the Marquis, now dressed up to the nines, and fell in love with him.

Meanwhile Puss ran ahead. Soon he came to a field where some men were mowing grass. "Listen!" he cried. "The King is driving this way. When he asks you whose fields these are, you tell him they belong to my master, the Marquis. If you don't, I'll have you chopped into little pieces!"

Then Puss ran on a little further and came to a field where some men were cutting wheat. He repeated his instructions. Then on he ran again, and whenever he met anyone, he told them the same thing. At last he came to the Ogre's castle.

Slowly the King's carriage followed in Puss's tracks. Each time he came to a group of workers, the King asked them, "Whose are these fields, my good men?" Of course, he always got the same answer! The King was amazed at how much land the Marquis owned. (And so was Puss's master!)

Meanwhile Puss was very busy at the castle. "Ogre," he said, hiding a shudder at the Ogre's bad breath, "I've heard that you have the most amazing magical powers."

"Well, yes," said the Ogre modestly.

"For instance," Puss went on, "I've heard you can change yourself into a lion." In a flash the Ogre changed himself, and Puss fled to the top of a wardrobe, out of harm's way. When the Ogre had returned to normal, Puss came down. "Brilliant!" he said. "But changing into something small, like a mouse, must be impossible for a big fellow like you!"

"Impossible?" laughed the Ogre. "I can do anything!" In a flash he changed into a mouse. And… Puss ate him.

Seconds later the King arrived at the Ogre's castle. You can guess who owned the castle now! Puss met the carriage at the castle gates. "Come this way," he said. "A feast awaits you." (The Ogre had been going to invite a few friends round!)

By the end of the day, Puss's master, the Marquis, was engaged to the Princess. And by the end of the week, they were married. And Puss? Well, he lived to a ripe old age, using up every one of his nine lives, and he never needed to hunt a mouse again—but sometimes he did, just for the sheer fun of it!

The Twelve Dancing Princesses

There was once a handsome young man called Michael whose job was looking after the villagers' cows. All the local girls thought he was marvellous, but Michael didn't want to marry one of them. Come what may, he was determined to marry a princess.

Then one day a beautiful lady came to him in a dream. "Michael," she said, "go to the castle of Belœil. Find your princess there."

When he told the villagers, they jeered, "Cowherds don't marry princesses!" But Michael believed his dream. Next morning he set off to seek his fortune.

As it happened, he couldn't have gone to the castle at a better time, for something strange was happening there. The King's twelve beautiful daughters all slept in the same room, which was locked and bolted each night at bedtime. Yet in the morning the Princesses were as tired as if they'd been up all night. Even more mysteriously, the soles of their dancing shoes were worn out each morning.

The Princesses said, "All we do is sleep!"

But the King didn't believe that. He announced that if any prince discovered their secret, he could choose one of the Princesses for his bride. Prince after prince had been locked in with the Princesses. None of them had ever been seen again.

When he reached the castle, Michael got a job as a gardener. One of his duties was to give the Princesses a bouquet of flowers each morning. As soon as Michael set eyes on the youngest Princess, he knew that she was the one for him. He could tell she liked the look of him too, even though he was only a gardener.

That night he had another dream. The lady told him to plant two trees. When they grew they would grant him any wish.

Strangely enough, two young trees were by his side when he woke. He planted them and as soon as they'd grown, he said, "Make me invisible!"

His wish was granted. That night the invisible Michael hid in the Princesses' room. As soon as the door had been locked, the Princesses put on their party clothes.

Then the eldest clapped her hands three times and a trap door opened. Down a hidden staircase the Princesses went, with Michael following, but carelessly he stepped on the hem of the youngest Princess's dress.

Frightened, she called, "Someone is holding my dress!"

"Silly!" her eldest sister called back. "It caught on a nail."

At the bottom of the staircase was a grove of beautiful trees with silver-spangled leaves. Beyond that was another with gold-spangled leaves, then another where the leaves were studded with diamonds.

At last they reached a lake where twelve boats waited. On the far side was a castle. Michael climbed into the youngest Princess's boat.

"Hurry! We're getting left behind," she complained to the Prince who was rowing it. (He was one of the Princes who'd so mysteriously disappeared.)

"It seems heavier tonight," the poor Prince said, rowing his hardest.

In the castle, a ball was in full swing. All night Michael watched the youngest Princess dancing. How lovely she was! How beautifully she danced!

At three in the morning, the Princesses' dancing shoes were worn out. Back across the lake they were rowed. As they passed through the grove of silver-spangled leaves, Michael snapped off a spray of them.

In the morning Michael pushed the spray into the youngest Princess's bouquet. She saw it but said nothing.

The second night Michael followed again. Next morning the youngest Princess saw a sprig of gold-spangled leaves in her bouquet.

"You know our secret!" she said to Michael. She offered him gold not to tell the King. Michael refused it. In desperation the youngest Princess told her sisters.

"Throw him in a dungeon!" they said. But the youngest Princess said, "No!"

"Then let your gardener come with us," the sisters said. "We'll drug him like the others."

That night Michael had no need to wish himself invisible. Instead he wished for a magnificent suit of clothes so that he could look like a prince. He went with the Princesses to the ball and danced all night. Then, while they were resting, the eldest brought him a glass of drugged wine.

Now, Michael had heard all about this plot when he was invisible, but he could not bear to be parted from the youngest Princess, so he put the glass to his lips. He was about to drink, when she knocked it out of his hand.

"I don't want you to be like the others!" she cried. "I want us to live in the everyday world, even if it *does* mean I become a gardener's wife!" Bursting into tears, she threw herself into Michael's arms.

All at once, it was as though a spell had been broken. The real Princes suddenly remembered who they were and immediately asked the other Princesses to marry them. The Princesses had been enchanted by the magical world they had visited so often, but now they were overjoyed to find real happiness at last.

But the story ends even more happily than that, for when the King heard how Michael had broken the spell, he made him a prince too. So the youngest Princess didn't have to marry a gardener after all!

The Three Billy Goats Gruff

Once there were three brothers, the three billy goats Gruff, who lived in a land of high mountains and deep ravines. One day the brothers were out chewing thorns and thistles on a stony hillside and not enjoying their food very much.

The smallest goat, whose mouth was much softer than his brothers', stopped for a rest. He looked over to the hillside opposite and what did he see? The most luscious green grass a billy goat had ever set eyes on!

"Brothers!" he bleated. "Follow me!" Down the bank he bounded. There was a stream at the bottom with a bridge over it, and the youngest billy goat began to run across the bridge.

"Stop!" his brothers shouted, but far too late. In the ravine under the bridge lived a troll with the sharpest teeth and ugliest eyes in the whole wide world.

"Stop! Stop!" the brothers called, but the troll was already poking his head over the edge of the bridge.

"Who's that trip-trapping over my bridge?" the troll screamed.

When he saw the troll, the smallest billy goat trembled from the tip of his wet nose to the end of his feathery tail.

"I'm little billy goat Gruff," he bleated. "I'm only crossing your bridge to get to the young green grass on the other side."

The troll licked his lips with his enormous rough tongue. "Oh no, you're not!" he shouted. He began to wriggle his way up onto the bridge. "I'm going to gobble you up."

"But my brother's coming after me!" the little billy goat bleated. "And he's much *much* fatter than me."

The greedy troll immediately dropped out of sight and the smallest billy goat ran on over the bridge to the other side.

The two older brothers put their heads together to decide what to do, and a minute later the middle-sized billy goat Gruff rather reluctantly came down the hillside. *Trip, trap, trip, trap,* went his hooves on the bridge. Immediately the troll raised his head above the edge.

"Who's that trip-trapping over my bridge?" he screamed.

"I'm middle-sized billy goat Gruff," the goat bleated, "and I'm going across to join my younger brother."

"Oh no, you're not!" the troll shouted. He began to clamber onto the bridge. "You look fat and juicy. I'm going to gobble you up."

"But my other brother's coming after me!" bleated the middle-sized goat, at the same time trying to make himself look as small as possible. "He's much, much, *much* fatter than me."

The greedy troll immediately dropped out of sight and, with a sigh of relief, the middle-sized billy goat ran over to the other side of the bridge.

After a minute the largest billy goat Gruff started trip-trapping over the bridge too. *Trip, trap, trip, trap, trip, trap,* went his hooves on the bridge.

The troll could hardly contain his excitement at the meal he was going to have. "Who's that trip-trapping over my bridge?" he screamed.

"I'm big billy goat Gruff," the third brother bleated, "and I'm going across to the other side to join my brothers in the lovely green grass."

"Oh no, you're not!" the troll shouted. "No, no, no!" With his long hairy arms he pulled himself straight up onto the bridge. "I'm going to gobble you up! That's what's going to happen!"

318

The moment the troll's feet landed on the bridge, he realized he'd made a big mistake. Big billy goat Gruff was massive. His horns were longer and sharper than all the troll's teeth put together.

As the goat put his head down and charged, the troll screamed, "No, no, no!" He tried to dive back under the bridge, but far too late. The goat's horns tossed him into the stream and the raging water carried him away. No one ever found out what happened to him and no one cared!

The big billy goat Gruff trip-trapped proudly over the rest of the bridge and joined his two brothers. Perhaps he had a few words to say to the smallest billy goat for putting them all in danger, but certainly the Gruffs enjoyed the young green grass and lived happily ever after.

Hansel and Gretel

There were once two children called Hansel and Gretel whose mother had died when they were very small. After some years their father, who was a woodcutter, married again. His new wife came from a much better-off family. She hated living in a poor cottage at the edge of the forest and having hardly anything to eat. And she particularly hated her two stepchildren.

One bitter winter evening, when they were in bed, Hansel and Gretel overheard their stepmother say, "We've hardly any food left. If we don't get rid of the children, we'll *all* starve to death."

The father let out a cry. "It's no use arguing," his wife said. "My mind's made up. Tomorrow we'll lose them in the forest."

"Don't worry," Hansel comforted his sister. "We'll find our way home." Later that night he crept outside and filled his pockets with pebbles.

In the morning the family set off. As they walked, Hansel secretly dropped the pebbles one by one behind him to make a trail. At midday the parents lit a fire for the children and promised to be back soon. They disappeared into the forest but, of course, they never returned.

Shivering with fear, while wolves howled all around them, Hansel and Gretel stayed by the fire until the moon came out and lit the trail of pebbles. Quickly they followed it home.

Their father was overjoyed to see them. Their stepmother pretended she was too but her mind hadn't changed. Three days later she decided to try again. That night she locked the door. She wasn't having Hansel collect pebbles this time. But Hansel was clever. When they set off in the morning, he left a trail of crumbs from the crust meant for his dinner.

At midday the parents left the children as before. When they did not return, Hansel and Gretel waited patiently for the moon to light their way home. But this time the trail had gone. Birds had eaten the crumbs!

Now the children really were lost. They wandered through the forest, starving and frightened, for three days and nights. On the third day they caught sight of a snow-white bird in the branches of a tree. The bird sang to them and the children forgot their hunger and ran after it. It led them to an extraordinary house, built with walls of bread, a roof of cake and windows of sparkling sugar.

At once the children forgot their troubles and ran towards the house. Hansel was about to eat a slice of roof and Gretel a piece of window when a voice called from inside, "Who's nibbling my house?" Out of the door came the sweetest-looking old lady. "You poor dears," she said. "Come inside." Soon the children were eating the largest meal they'd had in their lives. That night they slept on feather beds.

But in the morning everything changed. The old lady was a witch who'd built her house of bread and cake to trap unwary children. She dragged Hansel out of bed by his hair and locked him in a shed. Then she pushed Gretel downstairs into the kitchen.

"Your brother's nothing but skin and bone!" she screamed. "Cook for him! Fatten him up! When he's plump enough he'll make me a lovely meal! But eat nothing yourself! It's all for him." Gretel cried and cried but she had to do as the witch said.

Luckily Hansel still had his wits about him. He decided to fool the witch, whose eyesight was not very good. Every morning she came to feel his finger to see if he was fattening up. Instead of his finger, Hansel pushed a chicken bone through the bars of the window for the witch to feel. "No good! Not fat enough!" she shouted. Back into the kitchen she went and forced Gretel to make bigger and bigger meals.

This went on for a month, until at last the witch's patience ran out. "Fat or thin, today I'm baking Hansel pie!" she screamed at Gretel. "Check if the pastry is baking properly." But Gretel had her wits about her too. She knew the witch meant to push her into the oven.

"I can't get my head in! I can't see the pastry!" she wailed. With a blow the witch knocked Gretel aside and pushed her own head into the oven. Gretel summoned all her strength, gave the evil old lady a huge push, and slammed the oven door after her.

Hansel was free, yet the children were still lost. They set off again through the forest. When they reached a river, a duck carried first Hansel and then Gretel across. Suddenly the children recognized where they were. They ran home as fast as they could.

How happy their father was to see them! He cried with joy as he told them that their cruel stepmother had gone back to her family soon after they'd been lost in the forest. He told them how heartbroken he'd been when he realized what he had done.

And there was another surprise in store for him. Hansel emptied out his pockets and Gretel her apron. They were full of gold and diamonds they had found in the witch's house. Now all the family's worries were over and from then on they all lived together in sheer happiness.

The Fisherman and His Wife

There were once an old man and an old woman who lived in a pigsty. They were so untidy and messy that the pigs had moved out long ago! The old man's hobby was fishing. One day he was sitting on the seashore fishing away to his heart's content when his line was nearly torn from his hands.

"Wow!" he thought. "This is going to be a biggun! I may even have caught a shark or a whale!" So he hauled away until the fish he'd caught (in fact it was a great big flounder) came flip-flapping onto the beach.

The old man had taken out the hook and was wondering how he was going to carry the fish home when the flounder said, "Now look here, old fellow, don't eat me. I wouldn't taste right. I'm not really a fish but an enchanted prince."

The old man was startled out of his wits. "Don't worry," he said. "I don't want anything to do with a talking fish." And he hastily shoved the fish back in the water and watched him swim away.

"Guess what!" said the old man to his wife when he got back home. He told her the whole story.

"You old idiot!" said his wife. "You mean you caught an enchanted prince and you didn't even ask for a wish?"

"The flounder didn't say anything about a wish," the old man said doubtfully.

"He might not have," his wife replied, "but he *should* have. Go back and tell him! Now! Off you go!" She pushed him out of the pigsty with her broom.

The old man was rather nervous but all the same he stood on the seashore and called,

"Prince Flounder, enchanted fish,
My wife Ethel wants me to get our wish."

At first nothing happened. Then the water swirled about a bit and the flounder stuck his head out of the water.

"My wife wants to live in a bungalow," the old man shouted.

"Go home. Your wish has been granted," the flounder said, and with a grunt he disappeared beneath the waves.

When he got home, the old man found that instead of a pigsty he and his wife were living in a bungalow. It had a bathroom and toilet, a proper kitchen, a fire in the living room and a neat little garden. His wife was purring with happiness.

325

All went well for a couple of weeks until one morning the old woman woke her husband with an elbow in the ribs. "A bungalow isn't good enough for the likes of me," she said. "Go back and tell that fish of yours I want a big country house. Go on, out of bed this instant! And," she shouted after him, "I want a butler too. And servants!"

The old man stood on the seashore and very nervously called,

"Prince Flounder, enchanted fish,
My wife Ethel has another wish."

The water frothed about a good deal this time but eventually the flounder appeared. "Go home," the fish said. "I know all about your wife's wish. It has been granted." And so it had.

And for a couple of months all went well. But one morning the old man was woken by the butler with a message from his wife.

"A palace?" the old man said. "She wants a palace! What else? To be King as well?" He was joking really.

"Yes, sir, I rather think that was the idea," the butler said politely.

For the third time the old man went back to the seashore. This time the waves beat so high on the beach that the old man was drenched before the flounder appeared, but even so the wife's wish was granted.

The old woman loved being King, and all went well for a couple of years until one morning a regiment of soldiers drew up beneath the old man's window.

"Your wife, the King, orders you on pain of death to go back to the fish," the general bellowed. "She wants to be made Ruler of the World. She wants to be able to turn the sun and moon on and off when she likes." The general stamped his feet and saluted.

This time a storm was raging on the seashore as the old man delivered his message. The waves were as high as mountains. At last the flounder appeared.

"Well, old man, what does your wife want now?" the fish demanded. Full of fear and trembling, the old man told him.

"Go home," the flounder commanded. "She's back in the pigsty already."

And you know, she and the old man are living there still.

Rapunzel

Once a man and his wife longed and longed for a child of their own. Then at last the wife discovered that she was expecting a baby.

One day the wife was standing at a high window, gazing down into a neighbouring garden full of beautiful flowers and vegetables, when her eye fell on a bed of special lettuces. Immediately it was as if a spell had been put on her. She could think of nothing else.

"I have to have some of that lettuce or I'll die," she told herself. She stopped eating and began to waste away.

Eventually her husband grew so worried that, one evening, he climbed over the wall into the neighbouring garden and picked a handful of lettuce leaves. This was a very brave thing to do, as the garden belonged to a powerful witch.

His wife ate the lettuce greedily, but the handful wasn't enough. Her husband had to go back next evening. This time the witch was lying in wait for him.

"How dare you sneak in and steal from me!" she screeched. "You will pay for this!"

The husband begged to be forgiven. He explained how badly his wife needed the lettuce.

"In that case," the witch said more softly, "take as much as she wants. But when the baby is born, you must give it to me." The husband was so terrified that he agreed.

A few weeks later the baby arrived. That same day, the witch came to take away the newborn child. She called her Rapunzel because that was the name of the kind of lettuce that the mother had wanted so badly.

The witch cared for the little girl well. When Rapunzel was twelve years old, she was the most beautiful child in the world. Then the witch took her to a high tower in the middle of a forest. This tower had no stair, just a tiny window at the top.

When the witch wanted to visit, she called, "Rapunzel! Rapunzel! Let down your golden hair!" and Rapunzel would hold her long, braided hair over the windowsill for the witch to climb.

This went on for several years, until one day a king's son came hunting in the forest. From far away he heard the sound of a lovely voice singing. He rode here and there among the trees until he came to the tower but he could see no way up it.

Haunted by the voice, he came back again and again until one day he saw the witch and watched how she got into the tower. Next day as it was growing dark, he called out softly, "Rapunzel! Rapunzel! Let down your golden hair!" A minute later he was with the girl.

At first Rapunzel was frightened, for she had never had any visitors except the witch, but the Prince gently explained how he'd heard her singing and fallen in love with her voice. When she felt less afraid, he asked her to marry him, and blushing, Rapunzel agreed.

But how was Rapunzel to escape? The clever girl had a brilliant idea. The Prince must bring skeins of silk each time he visited. Rapunzel could make them into her own ladder.

All went well and the witch noticed nothing until one day, without thinking, Rapunzel said, "Mother, why is it easier for the Prince to climb up my hair than you?" Then the truth was out.

"You wicked girl! How you have deceived me! I meant to keep you free of the world's evil," the witch raved. She caught hold of Rapunzel and cut off her hair, then sent her to live in a faraway desert place.

That same night, the witch lay in wait for the Prince. When he called out, "Rapunzel! Rapunzel! Let down your golden hair!" she let down the girl's chopped-off hair and hauled him up. The Prince was at her mercy.

"The cat has taken the bird," the witch hissed. "She'll sing no more for you."

In despair the Prince threw himself from the window. He wasn't killed, but the brambles below scratched his eyes. For several years he wandered blindly through the forest, weeping for his lost Rapunzel and living on roots and berries.

Then one day he reached the desert place where Rapunzel was living. Far off he heard a sweet voice singing.

"Rapunzel! Rapunzel!" he called. Rapunzel cried with joy at seeing her Prince again, and two of her tears fell on his eyes. A miracle happened, and the Prince could see again.

The happy couple travelled back to the Prince's kingdom, where they were received with great joy and lived happily ever after.

The Gingerbread Boy

Once upon a time an old lady thought how nice it would be to have a little boy about the house again.

"A boy?" her husband said. "We're too old for that sort of caper!" But he saw that she'd made up her mind so he said, "Why not bake a gingerbread boy?"

"What a marvellous idea!" the old lady exclaimed. She mixed up the ingredients, rolled out the dough, then cut out the shape of a gingerbread boy.

She gave him currants for eyes, a smiley mouth, a waistcoat and a hat. She even put buttons down the front of his waistcoat and go faster stripes on his shoes! Then she popped him into the oven to bake.

When the timer on the cooker rang, the old lady opened the oven door. But the gingerbread boy didn't lie still on the baking tray. He leapt straight out onto the floor and ran away through the kitchen door. The astonished old man and lady called to him to come back, but the gingerbread boy felt very grown-up and he shouted,

"Run, run, as fast as you can,
You won't catch me, I'm the gingerbread man!"

Down the road he ran, through a stile and into a field where a cow was chewing grass.

"Hey!" the cow mooed. "Stop and give me a bite to eat!"

The gingerbread boy thought that was really funny. "I've run away from a man and a woman, and now I'll run away from you!" Putting on speed, he shouted,

> "Run, run, as fast as you can,
> You won't catch me, I'm the gingerbread man!"

The cow ran after him in a rather wobbly sort of way, but it was no use. She couldn't catch him.

Next the gingerbread boy came to a horse. "Hey!" the horse neighed. "I'm hungry. Give me a nibble!"

But the gingerbread boy just laughed. "I've run away from a man and a woman and a cow, and now I'll run away from you!" He ran even faster, shouting,

> "Run, run, as fast as you can,
> You won't catch me, I'm the gingerbread man!"

The horse galloped after him but he couldn't catch him.

Next the gingerbread boy met some joggers panting along a path. "Hey! Stop!" they called. "We haven't had our breakfast yet!"

But the gingerbread boy just skipped past them. "I've run away from a man and a woman and a cow and a horse, and now I'll run away from you!" Running even faster, he shouted,

"*Run, run, as fast as you can,*
You won't catch me, I'm the gingerbread man!"

The joggers ran as fast as they could after him, but there was no way they were ever going to catch him.

Then the gingerbread boy came to a river and there he had to stop. He could run but he couldn't swim.

There was a fox in the hedge who'd seen all that had gone on. He came strolling out. "Don't worry, sweet little gingerbread boy," he said. "I wouldn't dream of eating you. I've already eaten a hen and a turkey and some leftovers from a dustbin this morning. Do you want to cross the river?"

"Of course I do," the gingerbread boy said, looking over his shoulder at the man and the woman and the cow and the horse and the joggers, who were getting closer and closer.

"Then hop onto my tail," the fox said. "I'll swim you across." The gingerbread boy hopped onto the fox's tail and off they set, leaving all the gingerbread boy's pursuers behind.

When they'd gone a little way across the river, the fox said, "My tail's sinking into the water. You don't want to get wet, do you? Climb onto my back." The gingerbread boy did so.

They'd gone a little further when the fox said, "Now my body's beginning to sink too. Climb onto the tip of my nose. You'll be safer there. Gingerbread and water don't mix, do they?" The gingerbread boy climbed onto the tip of the fox's nose.

The moment the fox reached the other side of the river, he flipped the gingerbread boy up into the air and down into his mouth.

Snap! A quarter of him had gone.

Snap! A half of him had gone.

Snap! The fox ate the rest of him all in one go.

And that was the end of the gingerbread boy who'd been too fast for the man and the woman and the cow and the horse and the joggers, but not quick enough for the fox!

Snow White

The snow lay deep on the ground. At a window of the palace the Queen sat sewing and dreaming. As she sewed, her needle pricked her finger and three bright drops of blood fell onto her embroidery.

The Queen looked at the drops and suddenly she had a lovely thought. "If my baby is a daughter, I want her to be as white as snow, as red as blood and as black as the frame of this window," she said.

Not long after that she gave birth. Her daughter was exactly as she'd imagined her. They called the baby Snow White, but sadly her mother died within a few hours of her birth.

A year later the King remarried. The new Queen was very beautiful but so proud that she couldn't bear the thought of anyone being more beautiful than herself. In her room she had a magic mirror. She would stare into it for hours on end and ask,

> "Mirror, mirror, on the wall,
> Am I the fairest of them all?"

Without fail the mirror answered, "Yes, O Queen."

But one day, when Snow White was fourteen years old, the mirror said,

> "No, O Queen, you no longer are.
> Snow White is more beautiful by far."

The Queen was so angry and upset that she couldn't sleep or eat. What was she to do? Then she made up her mind. She sent for the royal huntsman.

"Take Snow White into the forest and kill her. Bring back her heart and liver to prove she's dead."

The huntsman led Snow White away, but when he drew his knife the girl began to cry. He couldn't kill her. "Anyway," he thought, as she ran away among the trees, "before night comes a wolf or bear will do my job for me."

A young boar came by, so the huntsman killed that instead and took its heart and liver back to the Queen. The evil woman boiled them with salt and ate them and never knew the difference.

But Snow White wasn't killed by a wolf or a bear. As night fell she came to a little house on the other side of the mountains. She knocked, but no one answered. Plucking up courage, she went inside.

Here was a sight to cheer her up – a long table with seven places set and a row of seven beds along the wall. Still no one came, and Snow White was so tired and hungry that she took a spoonful from each plate and lay down to sleep on the seventh bed.

A little later the house's owners returned. They were seven dwarfs who worked in a silver mine deep under the mountains.

"What a beautiful child!" they said, when they saw Snow White.

When she woke in the morning, Snow White was terrified by the sight of the little men, but she soon learnt how kind-hearted they were. They asked her to keep house for them, and she agreed at once.

"Take care," said the dwarfs as they set off for work. "And don't open the door. One day your stepmother will find out that you're here and again try to kill you."

And very soon the Queen did go to her mirror. Imagine her horror when it said,

"O Queen, you are the fairest here,
But on the far side of the high mountains' wall,
In the dwarfs' neat and tidy home,
Snow White is still the fairest of them all."

Immediately the Queen sprang into action. Dressed as an old pedlar woman, she set off across the mountains with a tray of ribbons.

"Pretty things to buy!" she called, and knocked at the dwarfs' door. Snow White, who was looking out of the window, fell in love with the lovely ribbon the old lady held up. What harm could there be? She opened the door.

"This one, my pretty?" the Queen asked, as she fastened it round Snow White's neck and twisted and twisted. Snow White fell down as if she were dead.

And that is how the dwarfs found her that night. They cut the ribbon and slowly Snow White came back to life. It was her second escape.

Next morning the Queen went to her mirror. How angry she was when she found that Snow White was still alive. She disguised herself again and set off across the mountains.

"Pretty things to buy!" she called by the dwarfs' door. When Snow White saw the comb the old woman was holding up, she forgot all about the danger. She opened the door.

"Your hair is so beautiful, let me comb it for you," the Queen said. But the comb was poisoned, and Snow White fell down as if dead. That night the dwarfs removed the comb and brought Snow White back to life again. That was her third escape.

When the Queen went to her mirror next day, she found Snow White was still alive, and her fury knew no bounds. This time she knew that she would need her most devilish magic. She prepared an apple that was poisonous on one side only. This time she set off disguised as an old beggar woman.

"An apple for the pretty young lady?" called the Queen under Snow White's window. "It's free. No need to come to the door. I'll pass it through the window."

She saw Snow White hesitate. "Not worried it's bad, are you?" The Queen bit into the side that wasn't poisoned. "See, it's perfect." She passed the rosy apple to Snow White.

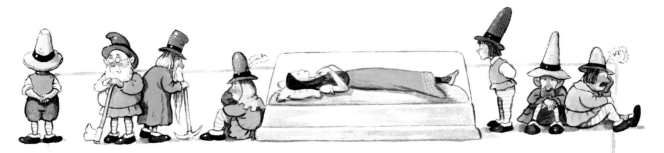

The moment Snow White bit into the poison, she fell to the ground.

The Queen peered in through the window. "Well, that's the end of you, my beauty," she said, "and good riddance." Off home she went. And next time she looked in her mirror it told her that, yes, she was the fairest of them all. How happy she was!

This time none of the dwarfs' skills could bring Snow White back to life. After three days they lost all hope, but strangely she still looked alive. Instead of burying her, they put her in a glass coffin and set it on top of a high hill.

Some time later a prince came to stay with the dwarfs. He saw Snow White in her coffin and immediately fell in love with her.

"Let me take the coffin back to my palace or I'll die," he begged the dwarfs.

The little men took pity on him, and agreed. But as the Prince's servants lifted the coffin, the piece of poisoned apple that had stuck in Snow White's throat was dislodged. She sat up, wondering where she was, and the first thing she saw was the handsome young Prince. It was love at first sight. Within a few weeks she and the Prince were engaged to be married.

One of the wedding guests was Snow White's stepmother. As soon as she entered the room, she recognized Snow White, but this time she was powerless. The servants seized her and the Prince banished her to a faraway land where she could do no more harm. From that day on, Snow White was the happiest girl in the kingdom as well as the most beautiful.

Thumbelina

Once a young wife longed and longed for a little girl of her own. Finally she got all her money together and went to a witch to ask for help.

"Is that all she gave you? That's just an ordinary barleycorn!" her husband grumbled when she got home. But the wife knew better. She planted the barleycorn and after a time it grew into a beautiful red and yellow tulip. Leaning forward, she kissed the petals softly. Very slowly and gently they opened out. And there, sitting inside the flower, was a tiny little girl. The wife loved her the moment she saw her.

Because the little girl was so small, only half as tall as a grown-up's thumb, the wife named her Thumbelina.

No one could have looked after Thumbelina better. The young wife gave her half a walnut shell for a bed, the petals of a violet for a mattress, and a rose petal for a blanket. When she wasn't sleeping, Thumbelina played on the table or listened to her mother's stories. She was very happy.

But one dark night, an old mother toad crept in through a broken windowpane and stole the little girl. "What a lovely wife she'll make you!" the toad croaked to her son, who was sitting on a lily pad in the middle of the stream. "Kark! Kark! Brek-kek-bex!" the son croaked back. He was as happy as could be at the thought of marrying Thumbelina.

But the little girl was very unhappy. "Please take me home!" she cried. One day, while the toads were away getting ready for the wedding, a shoal of minnows heard Thumbelina crying. They popped their heads out of the water. "Please help me," the little girl sobbed. The fish thought she was so beautiful that they gnawed through the root of the lily pad. It floated away down the stream.

For a week Thumbelina travelled along as happy as could be, enchanted by the wonderful sights she saw. But one day a flying beetle swooped over the water, saw how beautiful she was, and snatched her up. In great excitement, he flew to the top of a tree and called all the other beetles to come and look.

"We're going to get married!" he squeaked. "Us!"

But the other beetles, especially the ladies, didn't think much of Thumbelina at all. "Ugh! She's ugly! She's only got two legs! Where are her feelers?" they mocked. "She looks like a human!" In the end, the beetle got so tired of being laughed at for wanting to marry Thumbelina that he dropped her in a daisy.

For the rest of the summer and all of the autumn, Thumbelina lived on her own. She wove a hammock to sleep in from blades of grass and hung it under a shamrock. She took nectar from the flowers for food and drank the dew when she was thirsty. But then cold winter came. The birds flew away. The leaves fell off the trees. The shamrock shrivelled and died.

One day it began to snow. For tiny Thumbelina, each snowflake was like a shovelful of snow thrown in her face. She wrapped herself in a leaf to keep warm but it hardly made any difference. As she searched desperately for somewhere to shelter, an old fieldmouse took pity on her and called her into her nest.

"You can stay with me if you do the housework and tell me stories," the fieldmouse said. So Thumbelina was safe and happy again, until one day the fieldmouse's friend, a mole, came visiting. Then things changed. When he heard Thumbelina singing as she did the housework, the blind mole fell in love with her too.

"Come and see my house," he squeaked. "It's twenty times bigger than this."

Of course, the mole lived underground, at the end of a long, dark tunnel. He was used to never seeing the sky or the sun, but Thumbelina hated it.

"Just wait till you get there. You'll want to marry me straightaway," the mole panted, as he led Thumbelina and the fieldmouse deeper and deeper under the earth. Then Thumbelina stumbled over something on the tunnel floor.

"Never mind that," the mole called. "That died long ago." But Thumbelina stopped. She felt cold feathers. It was a dead bird. How sad! She put her ear to the bird's chest and just as the bossy mole shouted, "Hurry along! We'll be there soon!", Thumbelina felt the tiny flutter of the bird's heart.

The bird was a swallow who had hurt his wing and been left behind when the other birds flew south at the end of summer. All winter Thumbelina crept down the dark tunnel to take the swallow food and water. Slowly she nursed him back to health.

On the first day of spring, the swallow was well enough to join his friends who had flown back from the warm south. How sad Thumbelina was to see him go. The swallow had been her one true friend.

"At the end of summer," the fieldmouse said that night, "you and my friend the mole shall get married, Thumbelina. Your room is almost ready. The spiders are spinning your sheets at this very moment."

All too soon the summer had passed. On the day before the wedding, Thumbelina walked through the fields saying goodbye to the sun and the sky and all the things she'd never see again. She was quietly crying to herself when a voice above her called her name. Thumbelina looked up. It was her friend, the swallow!

"I've been thinking of you and all you did for me," he called, flying down to her. "But, Thumbelina, why are you sad?" he asked, seeing her face.

Thumbelina explained about the mole and the wedding. "Marry the mole? You don't have to do that!" the swallow cried in horror. "Climb onto my back! Come south with me and my friends. That's right – catch hold of my feathers. You're so small you won't hurt."

So, safe on the swallow's back, Thumbelina flew south. Sometimes they soared high over icy mountains, sometimes they skimmed low over plains and sandy deserts. Once they crossed a stormy sea and the spray from the waves reached up and splashed them. But all the time the air grew warmer, until one day they arrived at a place where there were many swallows' nests. Below, at the bottom of a cliff, was a field of beautiful flowers. The swallow gently put Thumbelina down on one of them.

"You'll be happy here," he said. "I know."

But Thumbelina felt sad. "Here I am again, sitting in a flower!" she thought as her friend flew away.

But what did she see before her? A young man, exactly the same size as her, was smiling at her from the nearest flower!

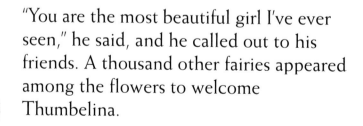

"You are the most beautiful girl I've ever seen," he said, and he called out to his friends. A thousand other fairies appeared among the flowers to welcome Thumbelina.

Within a month, the young man and Thumbelina were married and became the King and Queen of all the fairies. Little Thumbelina was happy at last.

346

The Princess and the Pea

Princes *must* marry princesses. There's no point in them falling in love with ordinary girls, however pretty they are. Everyone knows that, especially princes.

Once there was a prince who desperately wanted to get married. But, poor thing, he couldn't find the right princess. His mother and father the King and Queen did their best to help him. They even took their summer holidays in places where they met lots of princesses. When they got back they'd say, "Oh, by the way, we saw this lovely girl." The Prince would smile and say, "I bet she's a princess." And his parents would reply, "How did you guess? We've got her address. Why don't we invite her for a weekend?"

Unfortunately, the Prince never managed to fall in love. He *almost* fell in love. In fact, once he was engaged for over a year to a princess from Transylvania, but in the end the engagement was called off. Quite right too. They would never have lived happily ever after.

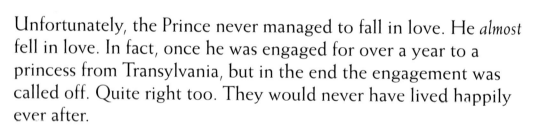

One dark November day a storm blew up. The wind lashed the palace roof so hard that tiles blew off like a storm of confetti. Trees in the royal park were uprooted, and the river burst its banks. It was so gloomy that the lights had to be put on by half past three (the King hated wasting candles), and it was so cold that the fires had to be banked right up. And the rain! It bucketed down. Not even the royal dogs, who lay sorrowfully in their baskets dreaming of sunshine and rabbits, wanted to go out.

348

About eight o'clock there was a knock at the
palace door. A servant was sent. He came back
and whispered something in the King's ear.

"Who says she's a princess?" the King
asked, surprised.

"The young lady at the door says
so, Sire," the servant said. "She
says she lost her way. She's
soaked through."

"A princess out in this
weather? Whatever next?"
exclaimed the King.
"Oh well, I'd better come."

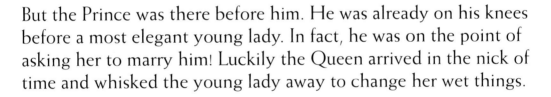

But the Prince was there before him. He was already on his knees
before a most elegant young lady. In fact, he was on the point of
asking her to marry him! Luckily the Queen arrived in the nick of
time and whisked the young lady away to change her wet things.

"Well?" the King said, when the Queen came back downstairs.
"Is she a princess? I bet she's just a pop star or a prime minister's
daughter like all the other girls he falls in love with. I'm
beginning to hate the word 'princess'. I didn't have so much
trouble falling in love with a princess in *my* day." He smiled
fondly at the Queen.

"I think I'll have to give her the test," the Queen said, "and hope
she passes."

"Test?" queried the King. The Queen explained. "A pea?
How can you tell if she's a princess with a pea?"
puzzled the King.

"You just wait till morning," the Queen
said, smiling.

Next morning the King paced up and down the sunlit breakfast room. "Isn't she up yet?" he asked his wife. "I hate people who lie in bed all day."

"Patience," said the Queen. "Let's see if my little plan has worked."

At last the young lady appeared. The King gasped. She looked awful, as if she'd never gone to bed at all. The Prince rushed up to her. "Darling! What's the matter?" he said. "Mother, didn't you give her our softest bed?"

"Of course I did," replied the Queen. "I put twenty mattresses one on top of the other, then twenty eiderdown quilts on top of them. What could be softer than that?"

"I feel black and blue all over," the young lady complained, as she dropped into a chair. "I'm covered with bruises the size of potatoes. That was the most uncomfortable bed I have *ever* slept in."

When he heard that, the Prince turned pale with fright. What if she left the palace and he never saw her again?

"But I did get a little sleep eventually," the young lady went on. "About four o'clock I couldn't stand it any longer, so I got out of bed and felt under the mattresses. You won't believe what I found." She held something out on the palm of her hand.

"A pea?" said the Prince. "Who left that there? I'll have their head off!"

"A pea!" said the King happily. "I understand now. Only a princess would be kept awake by a pea under her mattress!"

"Twenty mattresses," his wife reminded him.

So the Prince and Princess were married and lived a long and happy life together. And every night before they went to bed the Prince, even when he was King, checked under the mattress to make sure that no one had put even the tiniest pea there.

Little Red Riding Hood

Granny lived not far away, but to get to her cottage you had to walk through Bunny's Wood (though no one had seen a rabbit there for ages—you'll see why in a moment).

"Little Red Riding Hood!" her mother called. "Granny's still not very well. Put on your cloak and the pretty red riding hood she made for your birthday. Then pop over with this custard tart and pot of butter I've got ready for her tea."

So Little Red Riding Hood slipped on her cloak, fastened her riding hood under her chin, and set off.

"Remember to keep to the path in Bunny's Wood!" her mother called after her.

"Of course, Mummy," Little Red Riding Hood called back. "I always do."

She was only a little way inside the wood when there was a noise in the bushes and out onto the path jumped a great big wolf. Little Red Riding Hood nearly dropped her basket in fright, but actually the wolf seemed quite friendly. "Where are you off to, little girl?" he asked.

"To my granny's," Little Red Riding Hood replied. "It's the first cottage you come to at the end of Bunny's Wood. Granny's not very well. And my name's not 'little girl', it's Little Red Riding Hood."

"Sorry," said the wolf. "I didn't know. Tell you what—why don't I run ahead and tell Granny you're on your way? And, Little Red Riding Hood, don't stray off the path, will you? We don't want anything to happen to you before you get to Granny's, do we?"

Off skipped the wolf—just in time! For around the corner was a woodcutter. The wolf hadn't eaten Little Red Riding Hood there and then because he knew there was a woodcutter nearby who might come to her rescue.

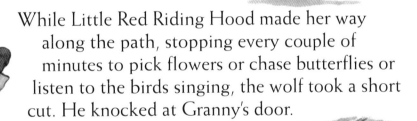

While Little Red Riding Hood made her way along the path, stopping every couple of minutes to pick flowers or chase butterflies or listen to the birds singing, the wolf took a short cut. He knocked at Granny's door.

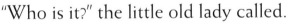

"Who is it?" the little old lady called.

The wolf disguised his voice. "It's me, Little Red Riding Hood. I've brought some good things for tea."

"The door's on the latch, my darling," Granny called. And in went the wolf. How hungry he was! He hadn't eaten for days. He swallowed Granny whole, from her head to her feet.

About ten minutes later, Little Red Riding Hood knocked on Granny's door.

"Who is it?" the wolf called softly.

"It's me, Little Red Riding Hood."

"The door's on the latch, my darling," the wolf called. "Come on in."

For a moment Little Red Riding Hood hesitated. Wasn't there something funny about Granny's voice? Then she remembered that Granny had a cold. She lifted the latch and in she went.

The wolf was lying in bed wearing the little old lady's nightie and nightcap and glasses. The sheet was pulled right up over his face and he'd drawn the curtains to make it nice and dark.

"Put the things down there," he said, "then snuggle up to me, my darling."

Little Red Riding Hood put the custard tart and butter down on the bedside table but she didn't get onto the bed right away. Something suddenly struck her.

"What great big hairy arms you have, Granny!"

"All the better to hug you with, my darling!" the wolf said.

"And what great big ears you have, Granny!"

"All the better to hear you with, my darling!" the wolf said.

"And what great big eyes you have, Granny!"

"All the better to see you with, my darling!" the wolf said.

"And what great big teeth you have, Granny!"

"All the better to eat you with, my darling!"

With that the wolf was so excited he couldn't contain himself any longer. He threw the bedclothes aside, jumped out of bed and swallowed Little Red Riding Hood whole, head first. Then he felt so happy and full of people that he lay back and went to sleep.

Unfortunately for the wolf, he was a loud snorer. A passing huntsman heard the snores. Thinking something was wrong with Granny, he crept into the cottage. He saw at once what had happened.

"I've been looking for you for months, you wicked creature," he cried, and he hit the wolf on the head with his axe handle. Then very carefully he slit the wolf's tummy open. Out popped Little Red Riding Hood and out popped Granny! They were completely unharmed.

Granny saw the custard tart and butter she'd been brought for her tea and, well, wolfed it down. Little Red Riding Hood promised Granny that she'd never be tricked by a wolf again. As she skipped home, she noticed that the rabbits had come out of hiding and Bunny's Wood was full of bunnies again.

"What a funny afternoon it's been," she thought.

Cinderella

There was once a girl whose mother had died. When her father remarried, his new wife brought the two daughters from her first marriage to the house.

These daughters took an instant dislike to their new sister. They threw everything out of her room into the attic. Instead of treating her like a sister, they made her do all the work.

Even when she'd finished her jobs, she wasn't allowed to join the rest of the family. Instead she had to spend her evenings by the dying kitchen fire, warming her hands above the cinders – which is how she came to be called "Cinderella".

One day, however, the stepsisters received an invitation to a ball at the palace. They were thrilled. Everyone knew that the Prince wanted to get married. Perhaps he would choose one of the ladies at the ball for his wife!

The two sisters immediately set about making themselves as beautiful as possible. Unfortunately this was very difficult as, unlike Cinderella, they were rather ugly!

On the evening of the ball, when her stepsisters had driven off, Cinderella sat in the kitchen quietly crying to herself. "What's the matter, Cinderella?" a voice asked.

Cinderella sobbed, "I wish I could go to the ball myself."

"And so you shall," the voice said. Cinderella looked up, startled.

A beautiful lady was standing beside her.

"I'm your fairy godmother," she said. "Now, no time to waste! Fetch me a pumpkin!"

Cinderella did as she was told. Her godmother touched the pumpkin with her wand, and it turned into a golden coach.

"Now six mice…" Cinderella fetched them and her godmother turned them into horses to pull the coach.

"A rat…" She turned that into a coachman.

"And six lizards…" She turned them into footmen to run behind the coach.

Last it was Cinderella's turn. One touch of the wand and her rags became a dress so magnificent it took your breath away. On her feet glittered a pair of glass slippers.

"One word of warning, though," her godmother said. "Be home by midnight. At twelve o'clock your dress will turn back to rags, your coach to a pumpkin, your horses to mice. You don't want the Prince to see that, do you? Now, off you go and enjoy yourself."

That night Cinderella was the belle of the ball. The ladies (especially her two stepsisters) admired her dress and begged her for the name of her dressmaker. The gentlemen all wanted to kiss her hand and dance with her.

But the Prince fell in love with her at first sight! No one else was allowed to dance with her after that.

The minutes whirled away and it was only when the clock began to strike twelve that Cinderella remembered she should be home.

"Come back!" the Prince called, but away she ran. By the time she reached the street, her dress was rags again. All she had left was one of the glass slippers. The other was lost, she didn't know where.

That night Cinderella cried herself to sleep. She knew that life would never be so marvellous again.

But that wasn't true. The other slipper had been found on the palace steps. Next morning the Prince went round the town from house to house, begging ladies to try it on. "If I don't find the beautiful stranger who wore it last night, I'll die," he said.

At last he reached Cinderella's house. The two stepsisters tried it on. No use. It just didn't fit.

Brokenhearted, for there were only a few houses left, the Prince was about to leave when he noticed the serving-girl.

"Madam," he said gallantly, "why don't you try it too?"

"Her? Don't be silly!" the stepsisters cried.

But the Prince insisted. He'd seen how beautiful Cinderella was. And of course the shoe fitted her perfectly. Spitting with rage and jealousy, the two sisters could only look on as the Prince knelt and asked Cinderella to marry him. And she did, of course!

Jack and the Beanstalk

There was once a poor widow. Her son Jack was a lazy boy, so they had very little money. One sad day things got so bad that the widow decided to sell the only thing they had left. She sent Jack off to market with Milky White, their cow, telling him to get the best price he could.

Jack was only part way along the road when he bumped into a funny old man. The old man eyed the cow and said, "My boy, I'll swap her for something very precious." He pulled five beans out of his pocket.

"Beans?" Jack said doubtfully.

"They're magic ones," the old man explained. That made Jack's mind up. He handed over Milky White and went home very satisfied with his bargain.

"Mum! Look what I've got!" he shouted. Jack's mother wasn't so happy, though. She threw the beans out of the window and a saucepan at Jack! Then she sent him to bed without any supper.

In the morning, however, Jack could hardly believe his eyes. Something was growing outside his bedroom window. He poked his head out. It wasn't a tree or a giant sunflower but a beanstalk that grew straight up into the sky. At once Jack clambered out of his window and began to climb the beanstalk.

Half an hour later he found himself in another country where everything was much larger. Across the fields was a very big house. A woman answered the door.

"What about a bite to eat?" Jack asked cheekily.

"All right," the woman said, "but if my husband the ogre comes, you'll have to make yourself scarce. He eats children."

Jack decided to take the chance, but he'd hardly sat down on the table when there was a roar outside.

"Fee-fi-fo-fum,
I smell the blood of an Englishman.
Be he alive or be he dead,
I'll grind his bones to make my bread."

"Quick! In the oven!" the woman said to Jack. "Nonsense, sweetheart, you can smell the scraps of yesterday's child I gave the cat," she shouted to her husband.

After his meal the ogre began counting bags of gold. That soon put him to sleep. Out sneaked Jack and stole a bag. He threw it down the beanstalk and scampered after. His mother could hardly believe their good luck.

But a few months later, all the gold spent, Jack decided to go back to the other land. Up the beanstalk he climbed. This time, however, the ogre's wife was more suspicious.

"Last time you came, a bag of gold went missing," she complained. "The fuss that caused!" All the same she let Jack in.

Very soon the ogre came along. *"Fee-fi-fo-fum,"* he started to roar. Jack hid in the oven again.

"Nonsense, angel," the ogre's wife said. "It's only the smell of that baby broth you had yesterday. Eat your buffalo pie."

After he'd eaten, the ogre shouted, "Wife, bring me my hen." His wife brought it. "Lay!" the ogre commanded, and to Jack's amazement the hen laid a golden egg. Naturally Jack stole the hen too.

By now Jack and his mother were well off, but after a year Jack decided to try his luck again. Up he climbed. This time he sneaked his way past the ogre's wife and hid in her copper pan.

In came the ogre. *"Fee-fi-fo-fum,"* he started.

"If it's that dratted boy again, he'll be in the oven, dearest," his wife said.

But of course Jack wasn't.

"I know he's here somewhere," the ogre rumbled, but although they searched high and low they couldn't find him.

This time after his meal the ogre got out a golden harp. "Sing!" he commanded, and the harp lullabyed him to sleep. Now Jack wanted that harp more than anything he'd ever wanted before. He climbed onto the snoring giant's knee, jumped onto the table and grabbed it.

"Master!" the harp cried. Jack jumped off the table. The ogre galloped after them. "Master!" the harp cried again, when Jack was halfway down the beanstalk. The ogre began to climb down after him.

"Mum!" Jack called. "Mum! An axe! Quick! Quick!" Together they chopped at the beanstalk and down it tumbled, ogre and all. He died instantly.

"Phew!" Jack said. "That was a close one!"

After that Jack and his mother lived rich people's lives. The hen laid golden eggs whenever they told it to. People paid to hear the golden harp play. It's even said that Jack married a beautiful princess. Maybe he did!

363

Beauty and the Beast

Once there was a rich merchant who had three daughters. Two of them were totally selfish, but the third, Beauty, was kind and loving.

One day the merchant received news that his ships had sunk in a great storm. He had lost all his money and was left with nothing but a tiny cottage in the country. The two greedy sisters hated it. They refused to do anything except lie in bed and moan. All the work was left to Beauty.

After a time, however, the merchant heard that one of his missing ships had reached port. Before he set off to claim it, he asked his daughters what presents they'd like him to bring back. The greedy sisters cheered up straightaway.

"Dresses and jewels!" they begged.

"And you, Beauty?" the merchant asked.

"A rose. That will be enough for me," Beauty said.

A few days later, the merchant sadly began his ride home. He was as poor as ever, for he had been cheated out of his money. As he entered a forest, the night drew in. It was dark and cold. A blizzard blew and the snow piled into drifts. Wolves howled in the distance.

For hours the merchant and his horse stumbled about, lost, until suddenly, straight ahead, a bright light shone from a magnificent castle. But this was the strangest of castles, for although there were fires in the grates and lights burnt in every room, no one was about. The merchant called and called. No one came. Eventually he tethered his tired horse in the stables and sat down at the castle's high table to eat the meal laid out there. Then he went to bed.

364

In the morning, he found new clothes laid out for him. Downstairs a cup of steaming hot chocolate had been put out for his breakfast.

"This castle must belong to a good fairy who has taken pity on me," the merchant said. "If only I could thank her."

As he was leaving, the merchant passed a bed of roses. "At least I can keep my promise to Beauty," he thought. He snapped off a stem of blossoms. Immediately there was a bellow of rage. From behind the bushes leapt a terrible beast, so ugly that the merchant almost fainted.

"You ungrateful man!" the Beast roared. "I saved your life! I fed and clothed you! Now you steal my beautiful roses. You must die at once!"

The merchant fell to his knees. "That rose was for one of my daughters, my lord," he said.

"I am no lord, I am a Beast," the creature snarled. He towered over the merchant. "And as for your precious daughters, go and see if one of them will save your life by coming to live with me. If not, in three months you will die."

The merchant rode home sorrowfully through the sunlit forest. At home the two sisters paid hardly any attention to the story of his terrible adventure. They were infuriated that he'd brought them no dresses or jewels. But Beauty was different.

"Father, let me go," she begged.

"You deserve to," the sisters said. "If it hadn't been for your stupid rose, the Beast wouldn't have wanted to kill our father."

Three months later the merchant returned to the castle with Beauty. All was as before: the empty castle, the meal ready on the table. Then, when they'd finished eating, the Beast appeared. Beauty trembled, for he was as dreadful as her father had described, or worse!

"Have you come here of your own free will?" the Beast demanded.

"Yes," Beauty replied.

"In that case your father must leave in the morning and never set foot here again."

So next morning Beauty was left alone. At first she cried, but then she remembered a dream she'd had. In it a lady had told her, "Beauty, your bravery in saving your father will be rewarded."

Beauty cheered up. Perhaps after all things might go well. She walked through the gardens, looking sadly at the rose beds, then explored inside the castle. Imagine her surprise when she found a door with her name on it. Inside, the room was exactly as she'd have furnished it herself, full of books and musical instruments.

"The Beast cannot mean to harm me," she thought, "if he intends me to enjoy myself so much."

Beauty took out a book. On it was written in letters of gold, "Here you are Queen. Your wish is my command."

"If only I could see what my father is doing now!" she cried out loud. And she could – in the mirror on the far side of the room. As the picture faded, Beauty felt less lonely and homesick.

That night at supper, the Beast appeared. "Beauty," he asked timidly, "may I watch you?"

"You are master here," Beauty said.

"No," the Beast replied. "You are the mistress. I will go if you wish." The Beast hesitated. "But tell me, do you find me unbearably ugly?"

Beauty didn't know what to say, then looked him straight in the face. "Beast, I have to tell the truth. I'm afraid I do."

When she had finished her meal, the Beast had one more question. "Beauty," he asked, "will you marry me?"

"No, Beast, never."

The sigh the Beast gave echoed round the castle.

Every night at nine o'clock, the Beast came to talk. Beauty found she liked him more and more. She even fretted if he was late. If only he wasn't so ugly! If only he wouldn't keep asking her to marry him! She dreaded having to refuse and hearing the haunting sigh he gave afterwards.

"You may not love me, Beauty," he said, "but you'll never leave me, will you? Promise that." For three months it went on like this.

Then one day Beauty saw in the mirror that her father was ill. At once she asked the Beast if she could go home to nurse him.

"Beauty, you must go," the Beast replied. "You know that I will die of grief if you don't come back, don't you? I am afraid that you will stay at your father's, but if you want to come back, just put your ring on your bedside table. The next morning you will wake in my castle."

"I will return in a week," Beauty promised.

Next morning Beauty woke in her own warm bed in her father's cottage. How overjoyed he was to see her! It made him better at once. That afternoon her sisters, who had both got married in the meantime, came round to visit. How jealous and angry they were when they saw that their father's favourite had come back.

"Listen!" one said to the other. "Let's trick her. Let's persuade her to stay a second week. Then the Beast will come and kill her." Instead of moaning and criticizing her, the two sisters rubbed onions in their eyes and pretended to cry at the thought of Beauty leaving. Beauty promised to stay another week.

Yet soon Beauty found that she was missing the Beast as much as she'd missed her father. As she slept she had a terrible dream, in which the Beast was lying cold and lifeless on the castle lawn. She sat bolt upright in bed. How could she have been so heartless? Quickly she pulled off her ring and put it on the bedside table. When she woke again, she was in the Beast's castle.

That evening she waited for him. Nine o'clock struck. He didn't come. Quarter past struck too. Suddenly full of dread, she ran through the castle and out into the gardens. The Beast lay on the lawn. She had killed him! Forgetting his appearance, Beauty threw herself upon him. His heart was still beating!

"I thought you would never come back. I tried to starve myself to death," he whispered.

"But I love you, Beast!" Beauty said. "I want to marry you."

Then something amazing happened. The castle seemed to become even more beautiful, more full of light. Beauty gazed around, then turned back to the Beast. But the Beast had gone. In his place a handsome young prince lay on the lawn.

"I want the Beast," Beauty cried. The Prince stood up.

"I *am* the Beast," he said. "An evil fairy put a spell on me. She turned me into something unbearably ugly. I would have stayed like that for the rest of my life, if you had not said you would marry me."

The Prince led Beauty into the castle. There she found her father and the lady she'd seen in her dream, the good fairy.

"Beauty," the good fairy said, "you have got your reward."

She waved her wand. In an instant everyone in the hall was transported to the Prince's kingdom, where the Prince's subjects greeted him with cheers and applause. Soon Beauty and her Beast were married. They became the happiest Prince and Princess that ever lived.

Goldilocks and the Three Bears

Once upon a time three bears lived in a house in the woods. They were called Tiny Little Bear, Middle-sized Bear and Great Big Bear. Their house, which they kept very spick and span, was full of just the right-sized things – bowls, cups, spoons, chairs, beds – anything you could think of.

One morning it was Great Big Bear's turn to get breakfast. He ladled the porridge into the bowls, just the right amount in each. But when they sat down to eat, the porridge was far too hot. The three bears decided to go for a walk while it cooled.

Two minutes after they had set off, who should come past their house but a little girl called Goldilocks. Goldilocks was a naughty spoiled brat who always did exactly what she wanted. She shouldn't even have been in the woods (her mummy had sent her to the shop to buy some milk). But there she was and she knew the bears were out walking. She tried the door. It wasn't locked, so in she went.

Goldilocks spied what was on the table. "Porridge!" She licked her lips. "My favourite!" She tried the porridge in Great Big Bear's bowl first. "Ugh!" she said. "That's far too hot." She spat it out.

Next she tried Middle-sized Bear's bowl. "Ugh! That's far too cold!" She spat that out too.

Last she tried Tiny Little Bear's. "Goody!" she said. "That's just right!" She gobbled it up. "Bother!" she said. "There wasn't much in there."

Then, because she needed a rest after all her wandering about in the woods, Goldilocks tried Great Big Bear's chair. "Hard as rocks," she said. "No good to me."

Next she sat in Middle-sized Bear's. "Miles too soft," she said.

Last she tried Tiny Little Bear's chair. "Just right," she said. At least she thought it was until her bottom went through the seat and the chair collapsed! Again she used a very bad word.

But Goldilocks was determined to get a rest. Upstairs she went and opened the bedroom door. First she tried Great Big Bear's bed, but that left her head too much in the air.

Next she tried Middle-sized Bear's. That left her feet too far up.

Last she tried Tiny Little Bear's. It was perfect! Without even taking off her shoes, she tucked herself in and went straight to sleep, dreaming of all the naughty things she'd get up to when she was older.

Meanwhile the bears returned home. They hung their coats up neatly and went to eat their porridge. Except, except...

"Who's been at my porridge?" Great Big Bear growled. "They've even left the spoon in it."

"And who's been at mine," asked Middle-sized Bear, "and done the same?"

"And who's been at mine, and eaten it all up?" Tiny Little Bear sobbed.

The three bears looked about. Someone had been in their house without permission and they didn't like that one bit.

"Somebody's been sitting in my chair," Great Big Bear growled, "and tossed my cushion on the floor!"

"Somebody's been sitting in my chair too," growled Middle-sized Bear. "My cushion's squashed."

"And somebody's been sitting in my chair and broken it," Tiny Little Bear said. He began to cry again.

"Sshh!" Great Big Bear said. "What's that noise?" The three bears listened.

"It's someone snoring," said Middle-sized Bear. The three bears looked at each other.

"They're still here!" Tiny Little Bear said. Upstairs they crept.

They went into the bedroom. "Somebody's been lying on my bed," Great Big Bear growled. "My cover's all creased."

"Somebody's been lying on my bed too," Middle-sized Bear grumbled. "The pillow's all out of place."

"And somebody's been lying *in* my bed, and they're *still* lying in it," squeaked Tiny Little Bear.

Great Big Bear's voice hadn't woken Goldilocks — she'd thought it was the wind roaring in her dream. Middle-sized Bear's voice hadn't woken her either — she'd thought it was her teacher shouting and that didn't frighten her at all. But Tiny Little Bear's shrill voice woke her straightaway.

She took one look at the bears standing in a row along one side of the bed, jumped out the other side and dived through the window. She landed in a bed of flowers only planted last week, knocked over the bird-table and ran straight out of the garden.

"She hasn't shut the gate," Middle-sized Bear complained with a sigh. "One of us will have to do it."

And what happened to Goldilocks no one knows. Maybe her mother just scolded her for not bringing the milk. Or maybe she did something worse, when she found out what Goldilocks had *really* been up to!

The Ugly Duckling

Deep in the bushes a duck was sitting on her eggs. She was bored with being on her own, so when the eggs began to crack she jumped off the nest with a quack of pleasure.

"Now I can get back to the farmyard," she thought, "and show off my new family!" She counted her cheeping ducklings to make sure they were all there. Oh no! One egg hadn't hatched.

"That's a large one left in your nest," another duck who was passing said. "I bet it's a turkey's."

"A turkey's egg? No, it's mine," the mother duck said crossly. With a sigh she settled back on top of it.

When the last duckling hatched, it was very large and ugly. To tell the truth the mother duck was rather ashamed of it.

All the same, her other ducklings were as pretty as could be and she didn't want to stay away from the farmyard another minute. She led her little family straight out onto the water.

"At least the ugly one swims very well," she said to herself. "So it can't be a turkey. Turkeys can't swim, can they? Perhaps it will get prettier as it grows older. Perhaps it will stop being so big."

Unfortunately the opposite happened. The ugly duckling grew bigger every day and all the other ducks noticed how different he was. Hardly a minute passed without him being attacked and bitten and jeered at. Even his brothers and sisters quacked, "We wish the cat would get you!" The chickens bullied him and the girl who fed them kicked him out of the way.

Finally the ugly duckling couldn't bear it any longer. He flew over the fence and scuttled away until he came to the place where the wild ducks lived. But the wild ducks thought he was ugly too and would have nothing to do with him.

So the duckling became the loneliest creature in the world. Even the little birds from the trees and hedges flew away when he came near. "It's because I'm so ugly," he said to himself.

He wandered here and there, always on his own. Once he made good friends with two young wild geese, but they flew away to escape the hunters. Once an old lady took him into her house, but her pets, a hen and a tom cat, laughed at the strange bird for liking the water and not being able to lay eggs. So the ugly duckling ran away again.

The leaves turned yellow and brown. Snow-laden clouds hung over the land. One evening at sunset, a flock of tall, handsome birds with dazzling white feathers came out of the bushes in front of the duckling. They had long, elegant necks that swayed backwards and forwards.

"Wait!" called the duckling, but the birds spread their enormous wings and were soon high in the sky. The duckling couldn't help himself. He turned round and round in the water like a spinning top and dived to the bottom in sheer excitement. From his throat came a strange loud cry, so strange it frightened him. He couldn't forget those white-feathered birds. Whatever they were, he loved them.

It was a long, hard winter. Several times the ugly duckling nearly died. Once he became frozen in the ice and a passing farmer had to rescue him. But at last spring came and the duckling found that he could fly properly, not just flip-flapping above the water but soaring high in the sky.

One day he was testing his new-found strength when, below in a river, he saw more of the beautiful white birds. He did not hesitate. "I'll fly down," he thought. "Even if I'm ugly, I want to be near them." And he landed on the water.

Two children were throwing bread to the white birds from the river bank. When they saw the duckling, they called to their mother, "Look! A new swan! He's even more beautiful than the others!"

At first the duckling didn't realize what they meant. Instead he bowed his head in shame as the tall white birds turned to look at him. "Kill me!" he thought. "I don't care what you do."

Then, as he raised his head, he caught sight of his own reflection in the water. And he couldn't believe what he saw. His neck was long. He had beautiful white feathers.

"Welcome!" the other swans called. They glided towards him, not angry with him or full of hate like the birds in the farmyard, but bowing their necks gracefully towards him as if to say, "You're beautiful!"

"A swan!" he said in wonder. "I'm not an ugly duckling at all. I'm a swan!"

The Elves and the Shoemaker

There was once a shoemaker who was very
poor although he was a master craftsman.
Every day he seemed to get even poorer.
In the end he sold so few shoes that he
had no money to buy leather to make
new ones. At last he only had one
piece of leather left.

That night he cut out the leather and,
with a sigh, left it on his workbench
ready to stitch up into his last pair of shoes in the morning. As he
went upstairs to bed, he could only think that if a miracle didn't
happen he would have to sell his shop.

The next morning, when he opened his workroom door, the
shoemaker saw something extraordinary. On his bench stood the
most beautifully made pair of shoes he'd ever seen. He darted to
pick them up. He turned them round in his hands. He couldn't
have made them better himself!

That morning a rich man walked past the shop. He saw the pair of shoes in the window and liked them so much that he was willing to pay twice what the shoemaker asked!

Now the shoemaker had enough money to buy leather for two more pairs of shoes. That evening he cut them out and left them on his workbench. In the morning, to his great joy, the leather had been stitched up into *two* beautiful pairs of shoes. The shoemaker was able to sell them for enough money to buy leather for *four* pairs of shoes.

For some time, things went on like this. Soon the shoemaker's little shop became so famous that rich ladies and gentlemen from all over the country came to see what he had to sell.

But one day towards Christmas, the shoemaker, who was a kind-hearted man, said to his wife, "Don't you think we ought to see who's doing us this favour? Think how poor we once were and how well off we are now. Tonight let's stay downstairs with the light off and see who comes." So instead of going to bed, the shoemaker and his wife hid behind the workroom door. As quiet as mice they waited.

As midnight struck from the tower of the parish church, the shoemaker's wife nudged her husband. Two tiny elves, dressed in rags, were clambering up onto the workbench. They ran around looking at what work they had to do. Then they seized the shoemaker's tools and began. As they worked they sang,

> *"Stitch the, stitch the, stitch the shoes,*
>   *Fit for kings and queens to choose!*
>   *Dart the needle, pull the stitch.*
>   *Work, work, work, to make the cobbler rich!"*

Long before dawn they'd finished their work and slipped away.

The shoemaker and his wife got up late next morning. Over breakfast the wife said, "Think how cold those poor little creatures must have been! Their feet were bare and their clothes were just rags. It made me shiver just to look at them. Don't you think we ought to make them a present to say 'thank you' for all the work they've done for us?"

The shoemaker agreed, and he and his wife set to work immediately. That night they left the tiniest clothes and shoes you could imagine on the workbench.

At midnight, as the church clock struck, the elves appeared again. At first they seemed puzzled to find no shoes to stitch, but suddenly they realized what kind of presents had been left for them. With whoops of joy they pulled on the tiny clothes and shoes. Then they began to dance all around the room, leaping on and off the table, balancing along the backs of the chairs, and swinging off the curtains. As they played they sang,

*"The shoemaker has no more need of elves.
Now let him stock his own shelves!"*

With that they ran out of the door and across the churchyard. They never came back. The shoemaker was sad to see them go but he could hardly complain after all the work they'd done for him. And they seemed to leave a little of their magic behind them, for he and his wife were lucky for the rest of their lives.